L.A. Blues

L.A. Blues

Maxine Thompson

www.urbanbooks.net

Urban Books, LLC
78 East Industry Court
Deer Park, NY 11729

ISBN 13: 978-1-60162-307-2
ISBN 10: 1-60162-307-0

First Trade Paperback Printing July 2011
Printed in the United States of America

10 9 8 7 6 5 4 3 2 1

Distributed by Kensington Publishing Corp.
Submit Wholesale Orders to:
Kensington Publishing Corp.
C/O Penguin Group (USA) Inc.
Attention: Order Processing
405 Murray Hill Parkway
East Rutherford, NJ 07073-2316
Phone: 1-800-526-0275
Fax: 1-800-227-9604

01S3

Acknowledgments

Ephesians 6:12 *For we wrestle not against flesh and blood, but against principalities, against powers, against the rulers of the darkness of this world, against spiritual wickedness in high places.*

Hosea: 4:6: *My people are destroyed for a lack of knowledge: because thou hast rejected knowledge, I will also reject thee . . . seeing that thou hast forgotten the law of God, I will also forget thy children.*

First, I give honor and glory to Jehovah. I thank Him for allowing me to live long enough to have a second career, and for being able to look back on all that has been bad or good in my life, and still know joy.

Sometimes we do not write the story we intend to write, but the one we are called to write. For years, I thought I would one day write about my twenty-three years of experience as a social worker in the inner cities of Detroit, (my home town,) and then later the mean streets of L.A. (which is my present home residence.) But instead, I became fascinated with the voice of my character, Z, who is the child of a female O.G. Crip, and a product of the social service system. It scared me to have to go where Z's voice took me, but as a writer, I had to push beyond my comfort zone. I generally write historical or women's fiction, which examines the old dark secrets spawned in slavery. My stories are usually taken from an era when we, as African American women, repressed and hid our sexuality.

Acknowledgments

This time, however, I found myself looking at our present day ills through a set of younger eyes—eyes which I imagined were on the other side of my caseloads.

Hence, *L.A. Blues* is my first foray into crime fiction, yet told from a woman's perspective.

This story started back in October 1984, when as a thirty-something-year-old social worker, I rode with two LAPD officers, as part of the D.P.S.S. ERIC (Emergency Response in the Community) Project. We were responding to a case where my colleague and I wound up placing three children in the middle of the night. I've forgotten a lot of what transpired that night, other than the fact that I'd worked sixteen hours straight. This I do recall, though—a sight I will remember as long as I live—a young black woman's corpse, laying in the floor with a knife in her back. Her husband had stabbed her to death. That's why we had to place the children. This image has haunted me for years. Thus, unknowingly, Chapter One of *L.A. Blues* was conceived.

I've also been haunted by a fresher sense of grief—an overwhelming sadness I feel for the young black males murdered on the streets of L.A. and other inner cities, and the attendant anger I feel about this carnage. I cry for the loss of all this young potential.

At the time I penned this story in 2009, this situation had hit close to home. My nephew, Sanchez Thompson, had just been murdered in Detroit at the young age of eighteen, only four months after I closed my sister's eyes in death at her hospice bedside. To say I was numb and grief-stricken is an understatement. But out of this grief, I've emerged with a sharper appreciation of life. In fact, this grief not only gave birth to my story, but gave me a renewed sense of purpose. That is, to try to save or to protect the lives of the upcoming generation.

Acknowledgments

That's why I quoted the above scripture to say, Bloods, Crips, or Latin Kings, (or whatever set you claim), are not each other's enemies. Let your enemy be injustice, poor housing, poor schooling, discrimination, and unemployment. Wage war against the institutions that perpetuate the ghettos and disenfranchisement. Know that this is a spiritual warfare as well.

Let's face it. We're witnessing a modern-day holocaust and genocide when young people are killed senselessly and no one does anything about it. How can we have a domestic warzone going on, yet no one seems to care about it? How can Black and Brown blood run in the street, and there's no outcry? These are just some of my story's questions.

But, on the brighter side, this story is a tribute to the "unsung" good foster parents, many of whom I was privileged to work with throughout the years. I thank them for the safety they provided the abused or neglected children entrusted to their care. I thank them for the free meals, the shoulders to lean on, and the much-needed solace I gained during home calls, as I was a young working mother myself.

L.A. Blues is also an effort to commemorate all the foster children who will become or have become strong "over comers" like my protagonist, Z.

That being said, I thank my late parents, Mervin and Artie Vann, who were wordsmiths and poets in their own right. I thank you for building a strong root in me; for giving me stability during the turbulent 1950s and 1960s, which has prepared me for the economic climate we're living in now.

I thank Horace Thompson, Jr., my husband of nearly forty years. Before you were diagnosed with dementia, you told me many stories of your street adventures as a Detroit police officer and a L.A.P.D. officer, which informed this novel.

Acknowledgments

I acknowledge my adult children, Michelle, Maurice, Tamaira and Aaron, and my thirteen grandchildren.

I thank Carl Weber, Martha Weber, Natalie Weber, and the Urban Book family for giving me this opportunity.

I thank Dr. Rosie Milligan who is a publisher, mentor, sister, and friend, who read my rewrite of *L.A. Blues*. I also thank Lorine Calhoun (actress Monica Calhoun's mother) for her reading and input.

I thank my network/writer family, bestselling authors, Michelle McGriff, Shelia Goss, Monica Carter, Suzetta Perkins, Charlene Green, Roslyn Wych-Hamilton, Leola Charles, Tracie Loveless-Hill, Rosalyn McMillan, N'Tyse, Brian Smith, Tiffany Tyson, Rachel Berry, Yvonne Medley, Christine Robinson, and Leigh McKnight.

I thank Ella Curry of EDC Creations, for her excellent on-line promotion of my re-issued novel, *Hostage of Lies*, and I thank Pat G'Orge Walker, a sister/writer friend, for the referral.

I thank radio show hosts, Dr. Rosie Milligan, Denise Turney, Gloria Taylor Edwards, Pat Tucker, Cheryl Scott, Kejohnna Owens, Yvonne Perry, and Kimberly Kaye, for having me as a guest on their shows in the past year.

I thank all the listeners to my radio show, the Dr. Maxine Thompson Show, on the Artistfirst.com Network. I'm coming up on my ninth year of hosting Internet radio shows. Thank you for your continued support. Please keep those emails coming!

To all the book clubs who have read my books, such as the Ten Ladies of Literature, who I found out on Google, read my first novel, *The Ebony Tree*, I thank you.

I thank Carol Mackey of Black Expressions, Tee and the Rawsistaz Book Club, Book Remarks, and APOO.org

Acknowledgments

for your continued support of Black writers and your role in our literary renaissance. I also thank Sexy Ebony Book Club for featuring me on their website for Mother's Day of 2010.

I'd like to thank Verna Bartnick and the late Art Bartnick, who acted as foster parents for me in my junior year of high school in Traverse City, Michigan, when I became the first black student to attend St. Francis High. This was an experience, which changed my life forever.

Last, this novel is dedicated to both the young and adult children whose families have been splintered by any of the following: the foster care system, the prison system, domestic violence, murder, incest, alcohol, drugs or gangs in the community.

You can contact me at maxtho@aol.com.

You can find me on the web at:

http://www.maxinethompson.com,

http://www.maxinethompsonbooks.com,

http://www.maxinethompsonshow.com

At twitter at safari61751.

On Facebook as Maxine-Thompson

On Myspace/Maxinethompson

Epigram:

When the legend becomes fact, print the legend.

—The Man Who Shot Liberty Valance

"The murder rate is down in L.A."

(The media)

In this business, you've got to have a little dirt on you for anybody to trust you.

—Training Day

Prologue

The L.A. Riots
1
April 29, 1992
East Los Angeles, CA
Zipporah a.k.a. Z

"Gimme your money, Mamacita." The punk had a cobra tattoo coiled on his right bicep peeking out from under his sleeveless-leather vest. He poked his gun, gangster-style, directly in my face. Apparently, he was the spokesman for this group of gangbangers who surrounded me. His wool cap slid down close to his rust-colored eyes, and his scowled look was threatening. I was shook, but I tried to appear composed.

"I beg your pardon?" I asked, stalling for time.

"You heard me. Did I stutter? Don't scream or I'll shoot you." The middle one, who was of medium height and sported a menacing bald head with a tattoo on his neck, leaned in, and a vicious sneer curled on his lips.

My pounding heart echoed in my ears and a gush of pee streamed down my legs. Why didn't I see this coming? Generally, I had intuition when it came to danger. My stomach quivered and I clutched my Slauson Swap Meet Gucci knock-off purse to my chest to try to calm my galloping heart.

I tell you. L.A. sucks. If it weren't for his sinister words, I would've sworn dude's mellifluous Hispanic accent sounded like a song. However, this was no love song. This was a siren of danger. The group of predators, who, judging by their smooth faces, could have been anywhere from ages thirteen to nineteen, meant business.

See, this is what I'm talking about. Can't go nowhere and can't have nothing in L.A. Can't even be nowhere without some shit going down. This place ain't nothing but a bunch of wannabe gangbangers who think they own imaginary turf that really belongs to the city. I don't care what the TV says about Hollywood and the beautiful people living here, in my world it was different.

I couldn't believe I was being jacked right here in broad daylight, on Cesar E. Chavez Avenue. I thought if I worked in a different neighborhood, if I got away from Watts or Compton, I could escape the Grape Street Crips or the Piru Bloods. I wouldn't have to worry about if I wore red or blue. I wouldn't have to worry about no stupid-ass vendetta against my brother, Mayhem, a born-and-bred Crip. But I guess I thought wrong.

It was still light outside for early spring, but no one else could be found in the parking lot as I looked around for help. I was surrounded by beautiful jacaranda trees, which covered the parking lot with their crushed-purple blossoms, yet the world looked dark to me. A gust of wind lifted up the leaves; they circled around my feet.

"What'd'ya talkin' about?" I decided to play dumb. My heart's palpitations almost drowned out my words.

"Don't make us have to kill you," the baby of the group snarled, his voice cracking, he was so young.

"Mami, we seen you go in there and cash your little check."

I didn't respond as my heart sank. *Please, God, don't let me die.* Just minutes before, I pranced out of Dix's Check Cashing Place floating on cloud nine because I'd gotten off work for the week and just got paid. I could feel the crush of fresh money pinned inside my bra. Having hard-earned money was the best feeling in the world, next to my release papers. I was released three months earlier from foster care. My emancipated minor's release papers included my birth certificate, my social security card, and my California I.D., which would supposedly set me free on my merry way to adulthood—whatever that means at eighteen. I could've gone in another program, but I wanted to be grown and on my own.

I never worried about being alone in East Los Angeles, or El Barrio, as it was called. The weather was balmy, and you could smell the Santa Ana winds on the fringes with a little hint of smoke. I wondered if California was experiencing its typical wildfire season early this year. I appreciated my first real job, if you didn't count after-school McDonald's, as a waitress at Maria's Mexican Eatery. I generally brought home day-old, warmed-over tamales, wrapped up in my purse. I drove my hooptie across town on the streets, but couldn't risk getting on the freeway. It was cool. At least I was off public transportation and was able to get around town.

I still didn't respond.

"Did you hear me?" The medium-height one held up his right hand, then rubbed his thumb and forefinger together, pointing to my purse. "Look, we don't want to hurt you, but give us that dinero, mami."

As frightened as I was, I still kept on my game face. "I 'on't got no money." I spoke in the vernacular I was used to before my foster mother, Shirley, taught me how to enunciate and speak "proper English."

My lead attacker grabbed my purse, and snatched it open, dropping my tamales to the ground. When he didn't see any money inside, he flung it back at me. My purse hit me in the breast and almost knocked the wind out of me. I winced in pain as he growled in a grimace of disgust. "We don't believe you."

They began to speak in Spanish among themselves. Fortunately, language was no barrier for me since my current roommate and former foster sister of eight years, Chica, a Latina, taught me Spanish. Plus, my late father, who was part Spanish, although he was black and came from Belize, only spoke to me in Spanish when I was a little girl. Even when my attackers were kibitzing among themselves in their native tongue, I understood them clearly.

"Let's check her car."

"Go 'head." I spoke back in Spanish and tried to front like I wasn't afraid of anything. At eighteen, I'd already seen it all.

They followed me to my hooptie, which, unfortunately was the only car parked in the lot. The taller one handed the burner to the medium-height one.

"Yeah, mami, you sho' is fine," the taller one said as he cracked open my car door. "I almost hate to rob you."

"Roberto, shut the fuck up," the short one snapped.

"Stoopid, don't use my name." Roberto came up out the car and slapped shorty upside his head, reminding me of *The Three Stooges*.

Meantime, the medium boy stood guard, still holding the gun and looking out for the police, while Roberto scoured my car.

"Bet' be glad this ain't no initiation day," shorty mumbled. I guess he was embarrassed that Roberto slapped him upside his head.

For a split second, I almost considered giving up my secret hiding stash.

I understood what initiation meant; from what I knew personally and from what I heard on the streets, my oldest brother Mayhem had outed more people since he'd been ten than I dared to even guess. My mother, Venita, was an OG who had been doing time for murder since I was nine years old, and I vaguely recalled witnessing a few drive-bys from when I was young.

If I hadn't been raised the second half of my life in a Baldwin Hills foster home, I probably would have been a second generation Crip myself, and perhaps money would've been no object because I would have been making that paper. But, as a working stiff, broke as I stay, no way was I parting with my only and last hard-earned two hundred dollars, plus the tips I earned as a waitress. After they searched under my raggedy floor mats, which covered the hole in the floor, under the towels I used for car seat pads, and under the back seat and found nothing, they turned back to me. For a moment, a penetrating silence filled the air.

"We should rape you," Roberto said. Suddenly, a shift in the current of their intentions flashed as their eyes beamed hard with lust.

"Yeah, let's pull a train on her, ese," Shorty jumped in.

I never took my eyes off the burner. I had to think fast. Should I give up the money? No, I decided I needed my little hard-earned money. I didn't know where my bravado came from, but I did know my younger brother, Diggity, age ten, and my nine-year-old baby sister, Rychee, as we called Righteousness, who was born while my mother was in prison, were depending on me to come visit them in their different foster homes over the upcoming weekend. They always looked for gifts.

Speaking in the broken Spanish I learned from my father, I challenged,

"Go ahead, Papi. Knock yourself out."

The shorter one's neck craned around, suspiciously. "What did you say? You serious?"

"Yeah, which one first?" I slid my hands down in a sexy, provocative manner between my long, sinewy legs that showed through my polyester uniform. Although I was thin at five-foot-nine, I was shapely. "Come on and get it. Give it to me. Hey, I ain't got all day."

"What the fuck?" Roberto threw his hands up, holding the other two back. "Wait a minute. You're too eager."

I wiggled my fingers in the air like a prostitute on the stroll flagging down a john. "That's right. I'm only HIV positive, but take your chances, *Papi*? Who's 'gon go first? Hurry up. Let's get it on." I even shimmied my shoulders.

"This bitch is *loco*." Roberto looked revolted, circling his right finger around his ear. He spit through the gap in his teeth in disgust.

"*¿Que paso?*" A strange voice interrupted my would-be attackers.

I glanced up and was surprised to see a stranger who seemingly appeared out of nowhere. He was a slightly older Mexican guy. I became even more afraid because I didn't know what to expect. Would he make my situation worse?

The stranger continued in a swift barrage of Spanish. "Holmes, leave her alone. She's a civilian. She's not the enemy. They're the ones in Simi Valley who started this mess. Remember *La Familia*."

Intuitively, I understood this young man seemed to have some type of power over the group. The three young men withdrew and slinked away like snakes going under rocks. Something about this dude oozed with confidence and swagger.

"What mess?" I wondered.

"Ah, fah-get it," Roberto said and he and the other two turned and swaggered off together. "She ain't worth it. No way. HIV puta."

I swallowed a humongous gob of saliva-laced fear and tried to hide my sigh of relief. Meantime, my good Samaritan stood, arms crossed on his chest, studying me. For the first time, I actually saw him. He looked like an olive-skinned gangbanger. Heavily tattooed himself, this guy had a cobra snake on his neck, a shock of wavy hair which fell over his left eye, yet there was a seriousness about him. He seemed to be just a bit older than the rest of the group, but they seemed to know, respect and even fear him. A leadership quality glowed in his face. It was as if he were the general in an army. On the one hand, he seemed at home, but on the other, he seemed kind of out of place with the environment that he was in. What did he mean by *"La Familia?"* I wondered.

After the young men retreated and were safely out of my view, I threw up a birdie toward their backs. *"Chillitos!"* I hissed, mean-mugging my would-be assailants. I stooped down and picked up my tamales which were wrapped in cellophane and brushed the dirt off them, then slipped them back in my purse.

"You really have a lot of gonads for a girl." My Good Samaritan chuckled. I didn't understand what he meant. He stood with his arms folded, looking bemused, as I clambered into my car.

"What's that?"

"Balls. You got balls like a man."

I could've told my savior a thing or two. He just didn't know. My mother, Venita, was one of the baddest female Crips back in her day. I'd seen her fight with men and the police just like she was a man. And she could shoot. My older brother, Mayhem, had been Cripping since he was eight and he'd taught me how to shoot a .22 when I was only eight years old. If I wanted him to cancel somebody, it wouldn't be nothing but a word for him to drop a Cholo, so maybe that's where my nerve came from. I don't know.

My savior continued to study me as I tried to start Old Nelly, my 1975 Mercury. Click click. Nelly wouldn't turn over. That's what I get for buying a used car. "I don't have AAA. . . . Jeez . . ." My mouth twisted to the side in distress. Just when I thought I was out the frying pan, I was in the fire.

Dude still had this amused smirk on his face, but he uncrossed his arms. "I don't have any cables. Maybe I can bring my boy back later and check on it, but it's getting late. How 'bout if I drop you off?" He nodded towards his car, which he had pulled into the parking lot.

"Well . . ." I thought about all the newsflashes about young girls last seen climbing in a stranger's car, who were later found in the Mojave Desert. I hesitated.

"Look. If I meant you some harm I could've helped those fools."

"Well, I don't know. It's kind of rough where I live."

"Any rougher than here?" He raised his hand in a flourish, taking in all of East Los Angeles.

"Where do you live?"

"Jordan Downs."

"I can give you a ride. I hear something's jumping off down in L.A."

"What?"

"It sounds like a riot."

2

The Los Angeles Riots of 1992, also known as the Rodney King riots, were sparked on April 29, 1992 when a jury acquitted four Los Angeles Police Department officers accused in the videotaped beating of African-American motorist Rodney King following a high-speed pursuit. Thousands of people in the Los Angeles area rioted over the six days following the verdict. Widespread looting, assault, arson and murder occurred, and property damages topped roughly US$1 billion. Many of the crimes were racially motivated or perpetrated. In all, 53 people died during the riots and thousands more were injured.
–Wikipedia

I climbed into Romero's silver Pontiac Sunbird. It wasn't anything fancy, but, unlike my car, it was neat and clean on the inside. The white leather upholstery was butter cream soft and smelled brand new. As I clasped my seatbelt, I said, "I don't know if this is such a good idea. Maybe you shouldn't take me home."

"Okay. Crip territory. How 'bout if I drop you before you get home, but close enough to walk? Name's Romero Gonzalez. Yours?"

When I rattled back in Spanish 'that will be fine,' and gave my name, he looked surprised. "Zipporah Soldano. Mmmm. Unusual name."

"My mother named me after Moses' wife. My father's last name was Soldano. "

"¿*Tu habla Espanol?* Where did you learn it?"

"My sister, Chica—well, she's Chicano. My father was charcoal black, but he was from Belize and I remember him speaking Spanish to me when I was little."

Romero looked shocked, I guess, since I was Lady Godiva dark chocolate. I sported a short, naturally curly hair cut, which was not kinky. Sometimes people say they were surprised at the texture of my hair. I never knew what they meant by that.

We drove through the streets, passing grocery stores painted like Easter eggs, cantinas, candle shops, paleta carts, and carts selling sliced mangoes mixed with lemons and cayenne pepper and papayas. We passed Mexican bodegas, brightly painted wall murals, vendor trucks known as "roach coaches", some graffiti walls marking gang turf, and turquoise and sage colored ninety-nine cent stores. Finally, we jetted on to the Santa Monica Freeway 10 heading West to the 110 Harbor Freeway.

"Thanks for helping me," I said, when I felt comfortable that he was really helping me. My gut told me I was safe.

"What are you doing on this side of town by yourself anyway?"

"I'm a waitress at Maria's Mexican Eatery. I know you think that's not much, but I want to buy a house."

"Oh, you want the American Dream?"

"Don't make fun of me."

"No, I think it's admirable. There's nothing wrong with hard work. I wished more people felt like you did."

"I've always wanted my own home. When I was a little girl I used to go visit my father and his wife at his house in Compton. I wanted to live with my father. He lived in a house like they have on TV. He had a little white picket fence and a white stucco house, which I hoped to have one day. Then I can get my brother and sister out of foster care."

I became quiet. My mind drifted to how I would spend my two-hundred fifty dollars of cash that I hid from my robbers. I was even thinking about moving to Torrance, if I could find a low rent area, if and when my Section 8 went through. Right now, though, I lived in the projects not far from the building I grew up in.

"Oh, where is your father now?" Romero's question interrupted my reverie.

The memory of my father lying in the floor, bullet wound in his chest, reeled across my eyeballs, leaped down in my throat and almost choked me, but I squashed it. "He died when I was young."

"Sorry to hear that."

"Were those Cholos?" I changed the subject. I was referring to my gang of would-be attackers.

"No, they call themselves Junior Mexican Mafias. They just a bunch of wannabes."

As we traveled south on the Harbor Freeway, passing colonnades of palm trees on each side of the freeway, something came on the radio about a group of Black men pulling a white truck driver named Reginald Denny out of his car and assaulting him. Romero turned the radio up louder. "What in the world is going on?"

The radio announcer's words gave the answer. "An all white jury in Simi Valley acquitted the officers of beating Rodney King. We are now beginning to see what looks like the beginning of a riot taking place at Normandie Avenue and Florence. This place appears to be the flash point area. People of all races are coming from all over to this cauldron of anarchy. Where are the police? People, stay in your homes."

"That's fucked up," Romero commented, shaking his head. "I heard something might jump off, but I didn't know it would happen this soon."

All of a sudden, a wall of fire like a dragon's breath flashed and flickered over the freeway, almost making us run into the Porsche in front of us. Romero hit the brakes in time to stop from hitting the car. A dark cloud rose up in the sky to the east. The air, filled with smoke and soot, felt like a furnace. Helicopters were circling overhead like buzzards, and the whirring sounds made the hair stand up on the back of my neck. I was petrified. Would we wind up trapped and incinerated right here on the Harbor Freeway? "I'm scared. Did you see those flames?"

"Let's get off of here," Romero said, "before we get trapped down here." He pulled up on Gage exit and we traveled Compton Boulevard South the rest of the way to 103rd Street just outside the entrance to Jordan Downs. I noticed crowds swarming up the street heading north. A few buildings in the neighborhood were on fire and the smell of soot permeated the air. The sun was beginning to sink to the west, and the day was growing grayer.

For a while I was quiet. My mind was on my younger sister and brother. Were they safe? Since I turned eighteen, I tracked my two younger siblings down in different foster homes, which were in Rowling Heights and Pasadena. Finally, I spoke out. "Can you tell me something?"

"Shoot."

"Why did you help me?"

"Just say I'm trying to turn my life around. I'm going to L.A. City College now."

"Oh, yeah? What you studying?"

"Criminal justice and psychology."

"Yeah?" I had no idea what either one meant.

"Yep. I plan on getting on the L.A.P.D." He nodded his head, as if in affirmation.

Suddenly "Don't be Afraid," by Aaron Hall played on the radio.

I hummed along to the line, 'Don't be afraid, girl.' Yet I was feeling even more afraid. Something wasn't right. What was going on in the world?

I noticed the cobra tattoo on his arm as Romero changed the radio station to a Spanish station. He also had one on his neck. "You used to bang?"

"Hey, you sure ask a lot of questions. Maybe one day we'll meet again."

I glanced away and kept my face as hard as an iceberg, but, like the song, I was no longer afraid—at least not of Romero. "I think you should let me off here," I said two blocks away from 103rd and Central Avenue. Romero nodded without saying anything. We exchanged phone numbers.

Later, after the smoke settled, when I picked up my car, I found he'd had it fixed. I never saw Romero again, that is, until years later.

Over the years that lapsed, sometimes I thought he was an angel I imagined.

3

After I scooted out of Romero's car, I jogged up to 103rd and Central, the mouth of Watts. I sprinted past the gang graffiti on the wall, past the community garden, past the glass-splattered streets and past the brimming crowds, until I got inside Jordan Downs Projects. Suddenly it hit me. Where were all these people coming from and where were they going? More people than I had seen in a long time were milling about on the streets.

A girl named Kenny, who lived next door to us in the same army barrack-style unit, flew by, eyes looking mad crazy. "Z, c'mon and roll with us."

I flagged my hand in dismissal. "No, I'm getting inside."

"Girl, we looting. Everythang free. It's a fire sale! C'mon!"

"I'm good." I waved good-bye. I looked on as Kenny leaped into a low-rider with four known Crips, their speakers blasting Ice Cube's "Kill at Will". They sped off, burning rubber like a mug. A tunnel of black smoke billowed up in the sky northwest of me and the wind made a swooshing sound. The loud roar of people shouting, glass shattering, and gunfire saturated the air. The wail of police car sirens blared in the distance. The 'whoop whoop' sound of helicopters hovering dangerously low buzzed in my ear. I could see the hysteria in people's faces as they stampeded through the streets. The smells of marijuana and liquor permeated the air.

I shook my head, as if to shake off my skin, which I felt like a stranger inside. I was walking against the crowd and everyone was heading in the opposite direction—toward the fire. I was just the opposite. I wanted to get away from the heat. I wanted safety.

When I made it to the apartment, I eased my key in the door. Although it partially opened, it jumped back because the chain was on the door. I was locked out.

I banged on the door with my fist. "Chica, let me in."

I heard her heels clackety-clack down the steps on the stair well. I figured she was upstairs and maybe she hadn't heard me knocking. When Chica finally unlatched the chain, she had this goofy look splattered all over her face. She slung her waist-length hair to one side.

Right away, I could tell Chica was high as someone on that shurm, primo, or PCP, or something, and she looked startled as a starved-out deer in somebody's headlights. I knew she smoked a little weed in the past, but for the first time, I noticed she was losing weight off her size six frame. Plus, she was wearing a man's shirt, which hung off her bare shoulder. Was she doing something stronger? I wondered.

"What's up?" I asked as I stepped in the door of our scantily-furnished apartment, looking around the living room, which led into our small kitchen. I was sniffing at this strange smell. Something wasn't right. "Why the chain on the door?"

"Oh, girl—" Chica's voice dragged. She sounded as if she was speaking from under water. She tried to wave her hand but it seemed like her hand was too heavy to hold up.

"Baby, who is that?" a baritone male voice called out.

I gazed up the stairwell and saw Dog Bite—one of the most notorious drug dealers in Jordan Downs—standing in Chica's bedroom doorway, which was at the head of the stairwell of our two-story apartment. He was wearing sagging boxer shorts and no T-shirt. He was buff since he'd just gotten out the joint, and he had tattoos all over his chest.

"Oh, it's Z," he said nonchalantly. "I'll be waitin' on you, Chica." He winked at Chica and licked his chapped lips. With that, Dog Bite strolled back into Chica's room.

"What the f—" I threw my hands up in disgust. I was so mad I spun Chica toward me, pointed my finger in her face, and called her by her real name. "Maritza, what was our pact?"

Chica stopped, a smirk written on her face. She cocked her head to the right, then slid her hand along the side of her face in a "forget you, forgot you, never thought about you" sign. "Girl, you still on that virgin shit?"

"No, it's not that." I paused. True, I was still a virgin, but apparently Chica no longer was, so what could I say? I cut into her to see if she was still the person I once knew. "What was our pact?"

"I know, I know."

"What did we say?"

When she didn't answer, I spoke for her. "We said we weren't going to let sex stop us from reaching our dreams." When we'd moved back to Jordan Downs from Baldwin Hills, we were about the only ones on our street our age without babies.

"Yeah, yeah. But see, Z, your dreams are bigger than mine. You want to go to college. I just want to go to beauty college. That's only a nine-month program." She started giggling.

"You know what?" I grabbed Chica by her shoulders and shook her up and down like a raggedy Ann doll. "You look like a fucked-out, used-up crack ho." I released her.

"Whatever. Me and Bite love each other. Try it, you might like it, girl."

"Not with that drug dealer. Oh, hell na." Suddenly I panned the room and spotted a glass pipe lying on our milk crate that doubled as a coffee table/dresser drawer. I got crazy mad then. "So yo' funky ass usin' that shit?" I went off on her. "Not the same shit that caused us to lose our parents, not the shit that got our brothers and sisters spread all over kingdom come. Not the shit—"

I sputtered, too stunned to continue. "Well, I be damned."

"Aw, fughetit, girl," Chica's voice sounded like she was speaking in a language called "glub-glub" under water, she was so high.

Without thinking, I hauled off and slapped Chica so hard across the face, she fell to the floor. I stood over her, fists balled up, ready to beat her ass if necessary. "I'll kill you before I let you turn out like that." My look dared her to get up too soon.

Chica just stared back up at me, holding her face in disbelief.

She slowly climbed to her feet, and was standing so close to me, I got a whiff of her body odor—bodussy. I began gesticulating with my finger. "And another thang," I added, "wash your behind because your ass stank. Better yet, take a douche since you so grown now." Chica didn't answer. She stumbled back upstairs into her room and slammed the door.

Feeling hopeless, I flounced down on our only piece of furniture, a used futon, and stared absently as the news showed images of the rioters in the street, burning buildings and looting, when suddenly the screen blacked out. Where were the police when you need they ass, I wondered. When the screen came back on, a television commercial for L.A.P.D. recruitment flashed across it, asking if you wanted a career in law enforcement.

I guess I was so sick of L.A., for the first time I actually paid attention to this Public Service Announcement. What had happened to me earlier that evening—almost getting mugged and gang raped—hadn't been my first involvement with crime. Yes, I was sick of crime. Maybe this was the answer. Maybe I should become a cop. But how could I do this? I was born into a crime family. Now, I'd like to fight it. The first nine years of my life, I grew up seeing crime as a normal way of life, but after being raised in a decent foster home for the last nine years, I didn't see crime as a good thing.

I still wanted to get Diggity and Ry-chee out of the foster care system to come live with me. I graduated in December, and then turned eighteen in January. I was late graduating from high school because I'd missed so much school in my early years, but I made it up after I got in Shirley's home and by going to summer school. When I was a sophomore, I met a teacher, Miss Golden, who enrolled me and Chica in a program called "I'm not your Victim," which turned my life around. It was for teenagers with parents who were incarcerated or on drugs. It started me to take going to college seriously.

Anyhow, it was too late for my nineteen-year-old brother, Mayhem, whose life was so entrenched in the Crips, that he was one of their leaders, and already a kingpin from what I heard. My brother had already had a few scrapes with the law, but somehow he hadn't been incarcerated yet. I gave up on him, but I had hopes for Diggity and Ry-chee reuniting with me and making something out of their lives.

Then an idea hit me. If I became a police officer, I could probably get my younger brother and sister into my custody without any problem. My family might be on the wrong side of the law, but I was going to be different. This was it. I would go out for becoming a police officer as soon as I turned twenty-one.

I glanced down at my wrist to check the time, then I remembered how my Timex watch and several other small items had come up missing lately. Something inside of me snapped. That's when I knew it was time to move. But where could I go? I had no father. My mother was in the pen. I didn't know what I was going to do, but no way was I staying with a crack head.

At eighteen, everything still looked black and white. I hadn't learned about the grays and the in-betweens yet, but right then and there, I decided as soon I turned twenty-one, I'd apply to be a Los Angeles police officer so I could get custody of my baby brother and sister. But I need a plan to carry me while I attended community college. I couldn't get sidetracked with Chica's mess.

I'd always hoped that I could get Rychee and Diggity out of foster care as soon as I turned eighteen, but, I learned the hard way, it wasn't that easy. First, they wanted me to have a job and a suitable place to live. I guess I was going to have to put that plan on hold. I never forgot it was my fault they were in the system in the first place. If only I had never placed that call that dreadful night.

The news flashed back to the burning buildings and the start of fires raging all over L.A., but they kept replaying the Reginald Denny scene where the gang of young Black men hit him in the head with the fire hydrant. Everything seemed surreal. Why were my people burning up our neighborhoods? I wondered.

Man, the world was going crazy. With television cameras in helicopters, crazy things were being reported as it happened.

I picked up the phone and called the very one whom Chica and I used to call "The Queen Bee," (Bitch) behind her back, and I mean she was a "B" in every sense of the word to us as blossoming teenagers. We couldn't really date. We had to go to church. She kept us in all types of activities such as modeling, cheerleading, guerilla theater, you name it. And, at sixteen, you had to work at McDonald's. Yeah, she was the original cock blocker. In spite of all my gripes against her, I called Shirley, better known as Moochie, which was her nickname when I wanted something.

"Hi, Moochie, what are you doing?"

Shirley sniffled and blew her nose into the phone.

Dayumn! I covered up my ear to keep her from splitting my eardrum.

"Sitting here crying, watching TV while my people burn down our city," Shirley answered. She sniffed again. "When I was coming home, I saw white, Asian, and Mexicans rioting, but all they're showing is my people on T.V."

It was times like this I remembered that Shirley used to be a Black Panther and was still a 'down-for-the-people' person. I murmured a few 'tsk tsks' sounds of sympathy, then I cut to the chase. "Can I come home so I can finish school?"

In one breath, I told Shirley about my plans to go to junior college until I was old enough to get into the police academy.

Shirley paused. My foster mother, a former Black Panther in the late sixties, who had morphed into this black middle-class postal employee who worked nights, got her degree in three years, then later turned school teacher, and who raised me from the age of nine, hesitated before speaking. I held my breath.

"No one told you to move out in the first place. Didn't I tell you Chica was too fast for you? Why did you let her get you geeked up to move out when I put her fast behind out?" She paused before continuing. "You can always come home."

Relief flooded through me. Home. Just the words I want to hear. In the life of a semi-orphan that word was a symphony.

I swallowed the lump in my throat. "Thank you."

"No thanks needed." She hung up without saying good-bye.

I heaved a sigh. If life were a lottery, then I hit it when it came to getting a good foster home. My peeps—my people—Chill and Shirley, treated me good when I was growing up the second half of my childhood, so when I hear the horror stories about foster homes, I knew I'd been blessed.

Now strange as they were as a married couple, (they'd slept in different rooms since I could remember), they were great as surrogate parents. There was never any physical abuse, misappropriation of the funds, or sexual molestation going on at our house.

In fact, when I was growing up there, adult foster children from years before would come home to Shirley's and Chill's rambling five-bedroom Baldwin Hills—calling them "Mom and Pops."

When I hung up the phone, I let out a sigh of relief. I could already see myself wearing my black and white police uniform. I just knew this was the right path for me.

1

(Fourteen years later . . .)
December 31, 2006
"I lived in Hell and I can tell you the address."

People always ask me did I kill anyone as a cop, but the truth was I destroyed my whole family as I knew it when I was nine years old. I would always wonder. Did I do the right thing? Some corridors in our lives lead us back to where we started, and we just unravel. No matter how hard we try to run, no matter how hard we try to hide, it seems as if everything comes back to the same place. Déjà vu. You can't escape the past.

Maybe that's why it seemed as if I'd been here before as I tiptoed behind my partner, James, in the narrow hallway whose indoor-outdoor carpet reeked of poverty, piss, and alcohol. We were in an apartment building with one floor, and we were headed to a back apartment. Our service revolvers, which were 9 mm Berettas, were drawn. I felt like I'd been here before, either as a cop, or in my life before I went into foster care. It was one-thirty in the morning.

Earlier, when the call came in to Southwest Division, it sounded like a typical domestic violence case. I just finished one shift, so when we got the dispatch, I decided to work overtime.

"Neighbors heard couple fighting. Children crying. Father may be holding the family hostage. Possible 187."

For cases like this, sometimes L.A.P.D. would call SWAT, L.A.P.D.'s Special Weapons & Tactics Team— particularly if this happened in the suburbs, but this was in South L.A., where unemployment and crime were high, and life and liberty was a cheap commodity. We were off of Hoover, around 52nd Street—Hoover Trades territory, I believed. Although we didn't have a warrant, we had probable cause to go inside—what was called exigent circumstances exception to the warrant requirement.

Across the nation, husbands were killing their wives, so it seemed to be becoming part of a Greek theater with this beginning recession. White, black, rich, poor, it didn't seem to matter. The domestic killing sprees were rampant. What made the husband do it? Or did something just come over him? Was being unemployed and not being able to take care of their family a rea- son to kill the whole family? Men and, in some cases, women, were doing it every day, so without saying it, we were afraid we'd find another case of a family being massacred.

Without warning, an apartment door swung open and a plum-colored woman with matching bloodshot purple eyes, wearing a tattered terry cloth robe, and a greasy headscarf, scurried out from her apartment, sputtering, "Officer. I called y'all seem like an hour ago. If she was white, I bet y'all da been here—"

"Save it—" My partner, Officer Okamoto, threw his hand up in the halt symbol.

"But, Officer—"

"Get back in your apartment," Okamoto barked. He turned towards the woman, his gun inadvertently pointed at her heart. "You're obstructing an investigation."

The woman gasped, placing her palm over her heart and without another word, she slammed her apartment door.

They say Okomato had a short-man's complex. I preferred to think he was just a little overzealous. When your life depended on your partner's quick reflexes, I'd work with Okamoto any day. He was my training officer when I was a rookie, and we'd been partners for the past ten years. He'd saved my ass a many time. The irony was he was a computer geek on his down time, when he wasn't getting wasted.

Unfortunately, this was the very job which I thought would be my savior, which in reality, had kept me working so many swing shifts I never did get Diggity and Rychee out of foster care. I don't know which came first. Working swing shifts or my drinking, but whatever the case, I wound up breaking my promise.

First, I began to anesthetize myself from what I'd seen on the streets with a beer at the end of the shift, and then, before I knew it, I guzzled down a short dog of Hennessy in the morning. Over the past ten years, I lost touch with my younger siblings, and they were now grown, adopted, and spread to the four winds. The last I heard, Mayhem was incarcerated in Folsom Prison.

Earlier that day, I received a letter, which was sent to Shirley's house from the Parole Board, saying my mother was being paroled in six months, but I was so angry at Venita, I didn't even want to see her. I hadn't seen her since they took her away in handcuffs with blood all over her shirt when I was nine.

Just thinking of my mother made me want to take a drink. I wanted a sip so bad I could taste it. I thought about taking a hooker from my small flask of Hennessey I kept strapped on my police belt, but I restrained myself. I was trying not to drink on duty since I'd been suspended for drinking on the job several times before.

Anyhow, I hated domestic violence cases when they turned 187 because they brought up too many memories for me. Truth be told, these cases could be more dangerous than a drug bust. So there we were, creeping down the dimly-lit corridor, into Hell's corner. I held my breath, heart flapping like the sole of a worn out shoe against my rib cage. With me piggybacking him, Officer Okamoto kicked in the door, and then stepped to the side. A rectangle of light fell into the dim hallway.

We stepped in, sweeping the area with our guns, we saw no one. Fortunately, there was no gunman. We also didn't see any children either. But I saw something else. "Oh, my God." My jaw dropped; my hand flew to my heart.

In the oyster moonlight, I saw the woman's blank eyes first. Devoted in her Hershey-grey skin, they held the ragged, blank stare of a jack-o-lantern's and right away, I knew there'd be no City of Angels for this woman after tonight. Although the smell of death was not in the room yet, the vibration of it was. It had an eerie other-worldly feel to it. Transfixed, I stared at the scene, as if I were watching a movie unfold.

Lord knows, over the past ten years as a police officer, there was little I hadn't seen. I'd seen a baby with syphilis in his scalp, I'd arrested a man who orally copulated his daughter because Mom was crazy and in a mental hospital and the twelve-year-old became the surrogate mother. Lord, I'd seen every atrocity known to man committed on men, women, and children, and I lived through my own nightmare I wouldn't wish on any man, woman or child, but this was different. It struck a chord in me that made me think of what happened when I was a child. It also made me know beyond a doubt, without "Mama", tragically, these children's souls would be up for grabs.

Over these years working the streets, I witnessed a few shootings, although I've never been hurt myself. But, there was something else about this woman's corpse that was different . . . as if she were an omen of something else bad to come. She also reminded me of what I wanted to forget—my past.

The woman's red gym shoe tread over and over inside my mind, perhaps because she only had the one shoe on. The other foot was bare with neatly polished, cherry-red toes. A brown grocery bag leaned against the wall by the door, as if in preparation to leave. A man's white shirt sleeve hung out of the bag. A lamp and chair were overturned in the living room floor. A hole in the linoleum, where the woman's corpse lay on her side, caught my attention.

"Knife wound," Okamoto said, then twisted his customary toothpick in the corner of his mouth to the side, and sucked his teeth. He swiveled away on one foot, and fired up a cigarette as if he'd said, "Nice day, isn't it?"

"Man, give me a smoke, too." Okamoto handed me his cigarette and I took a long drag. Meantime, Okamoto tucked his gun back into his holster, and lit up another cigarette, letting a gush of cigarette smoke rush out the corner of his mouth.

From habit, we switched cigarettes again. We stood still, contemplating what we were going to do. Okamoto took another long puff. "Guess we better call Homicide."

2

Although I didn't see the knife, I saw a pool of blood
haloed around the woman's back. She could have been
anywhere from twenty-five to thirty-five years old. I
turned away, sucking in the smoke, trying to keep from
vomiting. The room began spinning and the floor swayed,
feeling like the Northridge earthquake of '94. I was no
longer standing in this dimly lit, dank room because my
mind was somewhere else.

"Rise above it," my first therapist, Doctor Schmidt,
used to tell me. I felt my spirit lift above the scene. It
was 1983. I could still feel the blinding flashlight in my
nine-year-old eyes, see the pasty doughboy-looking
police man's face looming before mine, smell his coffee
breath, and hear his voice resonate in my head. "Did
you see what happened?"

My chest tightened and suddenly I couldn't breathe.

"Are you okay?" A voice snatched me back to the present moment.

"No. I'm cool." I sneezed to keep from passing out,
then covered my mouth.

"Bless you," Okamoto said.

I swallowed back the hot bile scorching the entryway
to my throat. My ears were logged as though I'd gone
swimming. I felt dizzy and ready to pass out any minute. I deliberately took deep breaths to center myself.

I caught a hold of myself when an emaciated man
with a craggy complexion appeared in the doorway. He

tried to peek around our shoulders to get a look at the body.

"The fuck you want?" Okamoto snapped. As a first-generation Japanese American, Okamoto had acclimated to the job and to the streets like he'd never grown up with Japanese-only speaking parents up in the Valley. "Who are you?"

"I'm a neighbor—"

"Get the fuck outta here and mind your own business."

I spun around and left, not looking back. After being a police officer for ten years, I guess I was becoming callous too, and smoking a cigarette was a defense mechanism. I squeezed the cigarette butt between my thumb and finger, and then stuck the leftover square in my belt.

Please, God, help me. I took deep breaths to keep from totally hyperventilating. I felt someone gently touching my shoulder. It was Okamoto. "Z, I can handle this if—"

"I got this." My voice cracked, and then the professional starch returned to it. "No, I'm okay. I'll talk to the children."

This was getting a bit too much for me, so I slipped down the hallway. I glanced over my shoulder, and not seeing anyone looking, took a quick hooker off the flask of Hennessy I had latched under my police belt. I downed a pint earlier. I wiped my mouth with the back of my hand, then popped a mint.

Out of the shadows, the woman with the greasy head rag appeared again. "Officer, Ma'am, my name is Florida. The kids are down here. I tried to tell that fool--"

"I know, Miss—" I cut her off. I couldn't take anymore, but I had to press on. "Miss, do you know what happened?"

Florida lowered her voice. "All I know is they started fighting around seven. It went on and on. The kids came running down here saying their daddy had stabbed their mama in the back."

When I first saw them, seated side by side on the plaid Herculean couch, faces blank except for their eyes entranced by the black and white TV, which flickered ominously into the dark room, my heart plummeted. I recognized the stare—the same one which probably had been mirrored in Mayhem's and my eyes when we were nine and ten—the vacant ravine—the landscape that childhood had deserted, never to return. These girls should be playing Double Dutch, singing "Rock steady, 'cause your team ain't ready," and the little boys should be out playing stickball, but no, they were now facing the unspeakable and the unthinkable—"Daddy killed Mama"—an affliction they would have to live with the rest of their lives.

The apartment's worn lentil-colored carpet had a nap which looked as if the sweeper was run daily. The middle child was wearing coveralls with one suspender hanging down loose. Her hair was shoulder length but looked as if it hadn't been combed for several days. Her thumb was stuck in her mouth as she twirled her top braid.

"Hello. My name is Officer Saldano. I'm here to make sure that you'll be safe." I directed my question to the oldest boy who looked to be about ten or eleven. "What's your name?"

"Shirrell." The little boy seemed unusually calm. His eyes were dry, but white salty streaks down his face betrayed his composure.

"How old are you, Shirrell?"

"Ten."

"And your name?" I glanced over at the older sister who appeared to be about seven.

The little girl pulled the only clean finger—her thumb—out of her mouth. Snaggle-toothed, she spoke with a lisp. "Sade." I knew she meant to pronounce it like 'Sha-day', but it came out like sa-day. She pointed her index finger at the youngest child. "Her named Starkisha." Starkisha, desperate for security, clenched her raggedy teddy bear.

"How old are you?"

"Seven and she four," Sade said.

I decided I might be able to get their vitals off the computer if the family was in the system or on public assistance.

Starkisha, who had braided extensions in her head, which were curled into esses and looked like a baby Medusa, peeled her eyes from the television set.

"What's yo' name?" she asked with a lisp through her snaggle teeth.

Before I could answer, someone knocked at the door. I glanced up and saw Okamoto. He stood silently and watched me, willing to jump in, if necessary.

Continuing the investigation, I was relieved the children knew their real names. I had cases where kids didn't know their birth names and would be headed for kindergarten. I'd say, "What's your name?"

"Boo."

"Your real name?"

"I said BooBoo."

But by no means, did this make these kids "BooBoo the fool-fool." Neither were they dull-witted or bovine. They knew their street monikers, which was all that mattered in their world. These children knew how to cross streets at stoplights at the age of two, knew how to lie to the social worker and say they'd had a full course meal for breakfast when their crack-using mother hadn't been home in a week, and knew how to list all the toys they'd received for Christmas when they hadn't received any. And Lord, don't put on a rap song. Those babies knew every word.

I turned to Shirrell, who was leaning on the armrest of the sofa.

"Shirrell, you're going to have to be a big boy tonight. Do you have a grandmother who lives in town?"

"Naw. She down south."

"Do you have any other relatives?"

"Unca Pookie."

"Do you know where he lives?"

"Yeah. He live behind the liquor store on the alley."

"Do you know the name of the street?"

"Naw. But I know where it is." Now this I didn't doubt.

"What is your mother's name?" It felt strange talking about the deceased woman as if she were still living.

"Mama."

The police report sheet read, "Jane Doe."

"No, what does your family call her?"

"Lady Bug."

Do the children know yet? I wondered. The youngest girl's lips puckered like a sewn together sleeve, and the oldest one was sucking on her thumb. Although Shirrell didn't know his mother's real name, he was a survivor. I had been there myself and I'd seen these children all my life. Sitting there, I wondered, *What will happen to these babies?*

3

After we interviewed the kids, Okamoto jumped on his Rover and called for back up, the supervisor, the homicide team and the coroner. The Emergency Response social workers weren't able to come on the scene so once Homicide arrived, our supervisor, Sergeant Stubbs, sent us off to transport the children.

When we left with the children, the coroner's truck was just arriving.

Squeezed into the back seat like a can of sardines, the three children sat flanked side by side on the drive to Uncle Pookie's house.

Absently, I shook my head. *Why hadn't I listened to my gut? This case was too close to home. I should have stayed home, instead of working this overtime on New Year's Eve. How did my foster father, Daddy Chill, used to say that? "Guts—always listen to your guts. People can smile at you and hate you, but your gut won't lie."* Well, tonight my gut was churning. Something, besides this horrible case, was definitely wrong, but what was it?

The problem was I was trying to buy my place in Venice, which was listed as a rental with an option to buy. I lived there for the past two years, and I was just now thinking seriously about buying the place.

"What grade are you in?" I asked Shirrell, who was sitting in the middle and, as the oldest had his arm around Starkisha and Sade, the baby. Starkisha's owlish eyes, bright as yellow egg yolks, looked as if she never went to bed before four in the morning, took in everything. An indelible print in a child's memory. I shuddered at the thought.

"Second grade," he answered. I remembered he was ten years old. "I got held back a lot," he added as a way of explanation.

"Oh, okay."

"What was that you were going to tell me about?" I turned to Okamoto just to kill time. When the shift started he said he had something important he wanted to tell me, but we'd have to be away from the station to talk about it. I knew he was planning to meet with Internal Affairs the next day. Then we got caught up on the second shift, and never had a chance to talk.

"Here's a key to my safe deposit box at National Bank downtown," Okamoto said, handing me over a key. "There's important information I want you to get if anything happens to me."

"What do you mean if anything happens to you?"

I slid the key into my duty belt, and closed the pouch. Before Okamoto could answer, Shirrell interrupted us. "Here it go. Oooh, there go Unca Pookie house!" Shirrell pointed out the window.

"Stop." I held up my hand in a halt symbol.

Okamoto nodded, then whipped the black and white over to the curb.

Sure enough, there was a single story bungalow behind a liquor store near 36th Street.

I had no doubt that Shirrell had often walked these five miles by himself from Hoover to this area.

My heart started pounding as soon as we pulled up in front of the house, and for the first time in a long time on the job, I felt spooked. I didn't know what it was. When Officer Okamoto let us out the car this time, my legs buckled in. I tried not to fall apart, but I was becoming more discombobulated with each second. A sense of alarm crept up my back.

We weren't sure if the children knew that their mother was dead and we hadn't told them. From the chatter among them, I figure they think she's alive. They reminded me of myself growing up—or at least they had a similar mindset. They were probably used to witnessing their parents fight. Domestic violence is what it's termed in legalese and is considered child endangerment. For these kids this was just a way of life.

The streets were even darker here than over at Hawaiian Courtyard's. The walk to the back house seemed to take forever. My heart beat louder with each step.

Uncle Pookie lived in a ramshackle backhouse, the porch leaning to one side, the step creaking as we climbed it.

I balled up my right palm. It was damp.

"I'll handle it." Might as well face my fears. I guess this was my way of running towards the fire.

After I knocked, a drowsy male's voice answered. "Who is it?"

"L.A.P.D."

Finally, the door cracked open, and a sliver of light shimmered and danced onto the one-step porch. Uncle Pookie, a dark-skinned man, scratching his three-day old shadow, appeared suspicious. He appeared to be about forty years old.

"What I do—I mean what's up?"

Officer Okamoto spoke in a stentorian voice. "We have bad news. Can we step in?"

After Uncle Pookie reluctantly let us in, we stood in the middle of a miniature living room. Two children were sleeping on both ends of the sofa, a thin blanket covering them. Uncle Pookie was wearing a wife beater with small holes in it over a pair of brown sweat pants.

A woman flew out of a back room, clasping her terry cloth robe, which was safety pinned together. Her sleep-filled, sable eyes widened with alarm. "Pookie, what's goin' on?"

"I dunno, MiMi." He nudged her. "Be cool."

My throat clammed shut and I wanted to scream, but somehow the sound remained lodged between my shoulder blades and my throat. I felt so conflicted, wanting to run, to not be there, to disappear. I despised the coward in me. Usually I was fearless, but I couldn't help it. This case forced me to relive the night that changed my life, and just like the little nine-year-old girl, I was again rendered helpless.

But, somehow, I pushed myself ahead. *Run to the fire,* I told myself. This was what my therapist once told me I had to do—face my fears. I cleared my throat. I had a job to do.

I spoke up before Okamoto continued. "Sir, is Lady Bug your sister?"

"Yeah."

"What's her real name?"

"Elizabeth Black."

"Well, sir. There's been a death." I paused. "Her husband killed her." I was amazed at how straightforward I was being. I guess, in a crazy way, I didn't have any reservation about being the bearer of bad news.

For a moment, Uncle Pookie's mouth flew open. He took in a gasp of air as if it were his last breath. There was such a long silence, I didn't know if he was having a heart attack. Then he pulled his elbows over his head, bent over, head in his hands, and broke down, sobbing. Mimi came forth and wrapped her arms around him. She began to softly cry with him.

"I knew it . . . I knew that fool would kill that girl!" he cried over and over. Finally, he peered up at us through red eyes. "He killed his first wife down there in Louisiana!"

In between sobs, I made out Uncle Pookie's words. "That Lady Bug—may she rest in peace—couldn't read her name if it was written in the clouds. Two years ago she left that fool down in Louisiana and then went back and got him. She been trying to put him out since last week."

So that's why the bag of men's clothes was packed by the door. Home sweet home. I scanned the faded wall pictures of a white Jesus, a sepia-toned picture of an older woman who could possibly be the grandmother and a portrait of Uncle Pookie's family. I averted my gaze and held my breath. *Lord, please don't make me remember. . . .*

"Sir, you're going to have to get yourself together so that you can tell the children.

"What is your name?" Surprisingly, my voice remained firm.

Uncle Pookie looked up, his face ravaged with grief, an old razor cut, creating a crag along his jaw line.

"Lawrence Mitchell."

"Mr. Mitchell, where does your mother live? I understand there's a grandmother down south."

"Louisiana."

I thought about it. I didn't want to have to place the children in foster care, if at all possible. It was late, and to find a shelter home at this hour would be difficult. The likelihood of them being placed together was null and void. I hated how my siblings and I had been separated from the gate so I didn't want the children to be placed in the system. "Is there any way they can stay here until we can get them to Louisiana? Of course, we'll have to do a criminal check—"

"Please bring them babies in here. They just like my own. I don't have no record."

I took down the names and social security numbers of the adults in the house: Lawrence Mitchell and Mimi Cross.

"I'll go back and have Okamoto run it on the car computer. If everything checks out, I'll get the kids for you." I was relieved to get out of this room stifling with grief.

I handed him the slip of paper. "Please run the criminal check on Lawrence Mitchell. We're going to let him tell them." I nodded my head towards the children sitting out in the car.

I paused, before continuing. "If he checks out clean, the kids can stay here 'til DCFS does an Interstate Compact on the grandmother."

We both returned to the squad car.

"Just wait a minute, kids." I turned my head and talked through the glass partition in the squad car. "You're going to your Uncle Pookie's. Everything's going to be all right."

Meantime, Okamoto ran the criminal check on the car's computer, and, unfortunately Lawrence Mitchell came back as one of several aliases. He had outstanding warrants, many drug-related charges, prior arrests, and even two strikes.

"Uh-oh. We won't be able to place them." Okamoto let out a low whistle.

I glanced over at the computer and saw a list of drug trafficking charges. A Racketeer Influenced and Corrupt Organizations Act charge, better known as a RICO charge. "Maybe I need to check this out."

Shirrell, Starkisha and Sade were still sitting in the squad car back seat, hands folded in their laps.

"Wait here," Okamoto said, stepping back out the car. Hot-headed as always, he bulldozed back up to the door and I charged behind him. "I got this," he said, throwing a hand up for me to follow behind him but to draw my weapon.

Like a cannon hurtling through the night, I heard an unidentified male voice bellow out, "It's the police."

The next thing I knew a barrage of bullets blasted through the air and all the oxygen escaped out my lungs. I felt a burning sting burrow into my upper chest, and then pierce through my shoulder. An unknown force pulled me down into darkness, but I struggled to remain conscious.

In a daze, I crawled back to the front of the squad car. I finally pulled my piece out my holster and fired back, but I was shooting aimlessly. I was not even sure where the bullets were coming from. I thought that they were coming from Uncle Pookie's house, but I wasn't sure. I crawled back to the driver's side of the car and struggled to open the front door.

"Get down," I whispered tersely to the children in the back. I heard the rat-tat-tat-tat of bullets flying all around me. "Stay down." It wasn't really necessary for me to say this. The children already had their heads ducked down, as if they were used to dodging stray bullets.

I finally made it to the mic on the driver's side of the squad car and uttered the worst two words in a police officer's vocabulary.

"Officer down!" I passed out.

4

"She's coming to." Shirley's voice was the first one I heard when I woke up.

"Nurse, she's conscious. Z, can you hear me?" I felt her hand gently touching my hand.

A wave of paranoia crashed over me. Who? What? When? How? Where am I? Suddenly I heard the sound of my heart monitor. Beep, beep, beep, beep. I peered over at the machine. Everything was blurry and it took a while for it to come into focus, but when it did I could read the blood pressure, which was 150 over 90, which was high for me. The smells of rubbing alcohol and disinfectant mixed with a musty odor.

"Where am I?"

"UCLA Medical Center."

Suddenly everything came rushing back to me in a whoosh, like a nightmare you can't wake up from.

"Where was I hit?"

"In the left side below your shoulder. An inch over and it would have hit your main artery. But God is good." Shirley teared up as she spoke. "It's a good thing you had on your vest."

"How long have I been out?"

"Three days."

"Where's Okamoto?"

Before Shirley could answer, I sniffed something. It was a sour and musty stench. It was me. I smelled funky.

"Dang. Don't they wash you up in here?" I asked, sniffing myself.

"Don't worry, Z," Shirley said. "I'll wash you."

As Shirley gently washed me, I glanced around and saw vases of floral arrangements. My eyes settled on a group of orchids, which were my favorites. Listening to the slosh of the warm water on my body, my mind drifted back to what I'd asked Shirley. "Moochie, you didn't answer."

Shirley acted as if she was deaf and dumb. She was quiet for what felt like the longest time. She finished washing me, and went to the bathroom, then emptied the wash pan. "Where's Okamoto?" I asked for the second time.

Shirley finally spoke. "He's gone." She paused. "Z, he's dead."

At first my eyes became teary and I rubbed them like I did when I was sleepy, but the next thing, I was boohooing loud, deep wracking sobs. All I could see was Okamoto and me getting wasted together on our off days. He was more than a partner—he was a friend. "It should have been me. I should have gone in first."

Shirley reached down and hugged me. "It wasn't your time. Only God knows when it's our time."

I thought about how they used to tease us, calling us "Cheech and Chong." How Okamoto kicked this racist cop's ass for talking about me. I wiped my eyes, and tried to stop crying.

"When's the funeral?" I asked between sniffs.

"It's tomorrow." Shirley plumped up my pillow, and eased me into an upright position. "You can't go. You're not ready for discharge yet."

I started crying all over again. Suddenly I felt paranoid and my heart started palpitating. "Am I safe here?"

"Yes, they've had police guards around your room twenty-four seven."

"How about the children we had gone to place? Are they okay?"

"Yes, they are fine. The children were placed in foster care, and the Uncle is in jail, so at least they caught the shooter."

"How about the husband who killed his wife?"

"He turned himself in."

Shirley's cell phone rang, interrupting our conversation, and she said a few, "Uh-huh. Uh-huh's." She hung up, and turned to me, trying to look upbeat. "I have a surprise for you. This should cheer you up."

I heard my hospital door open, looked up and, who should sashay in but my surprise guest.

"Hey, *mija*," a familiar voice called out. "I came as soon as I heard about it on the news." There, in front of me, stood Chica, whom I hadn't seen in years. She was rocking acid jeans, a turquoise halter top tied beneath her bosom, showing her stomach which sported no stretch marks, and she was back up to her regular size six. The next thing I noted was she'd cut her once waist-length hair to shoulder-length. This time it looked healthy. The last time I saw her and her hair was shorter, I knew she was going "crack head bald."

"Hey, girl," I responded as she reached down and hugged me. "Ouch." My face scrunched up in pain as she hit my bandages.

"Sorry, boo, " she apologized.

For a moment, I was speechless. In fact, I was kind of in shock. The last I heard, Chica was in the pen. In fact, when I last saw her, about six years ago, she was so emaciated, her front looked like her back. She'd lost her behind, which used to be J-Lo curvy. Clearly turned out and caught up chasing the elusive rock,

Chica had hit below bottom. Tricking. The whole nine yards. The last time we crossed paths, Chica was at Shirley's at the time, trying to hustle money under the guise of wanting a meal, and professing she was going to straighten up and go to rehab. I heard that lie before and I was so disgusted with her, I just shook my head and left the house, not even speaking to her. I was sick of her using Shirley.

During the L.A. riots, Chica got hooked on "the rock," had each baby taken by the County at birth and placed with Shirley, who even adopted the oldest two of the children. In and out of prison, over the past fourteen years or so, Chica had stayed involved with the wrong type of guys, including the whole downward spiral which came from that first puff off the glass dick with that notorious drug dealer, Dog Bite. I heard Dog Bite was shanked in a drug deal gone bad while he was in prison about ten years ago. He was the father of Trayvon, Chica's oldest son.

Seeing her now, here for me when I'm injured, I cringed at how judgmental I'd been. I guess I had been pretty harsh in my treatment of Chica. At the time, though, I felt like Chica had let me down. When we were teens, Chica was the better student. She liked to read, and could quote Shakespeare. We'd once had a pact to make something out of our lives, in spite of our circumstances.

Chica somehow, miraculously, gave birth to five precocious children: Trayvon, fifteen, Malibu, twelve, Soledad, eight, Charisma, seven, and Brooklyn, five, all bright, and all good kids, in spite of, or perhaps because of, their circumstances; which was the bright side of all of this. Trayvon, her only son who was the oldest, was an Honor Roll student and a high school sophomore basketball star. He was already being watched by NBA scouts. He had plans to attend Morehouse College in Atlanta after he graduated from high school. As the only only boy, he was Shirley's pride and joy.

You would have never thought Chica, who gave our foster mother pure hell as a teenager, would have been able to dump one, let alone five children on Shirley, but that's just what she did. Both Chica's mother and father had died in prison so there were no other available relatives. Thus, this was Shirley's second generation of foster kids she was raising.

Anyway, this was a new and improved Chica standing in my room. She still had the tattooed names of two of her three different baby daddies' on both upper arms, but she looked healthy. For the first time in years, she appeared to be clean and sober. Her eyes were clear and not blood shot. Her skin was not pimpled or sand-paper dry like the last time I saw her. She'd dyed her brunette hair a straw-colored blonde. She kind of resembled J-Lo now that she'd cleaned up her act. She was still a good-looking woman. I guess she had re-invented herself.

"When d'you get out?" I asked.

"It's a long story. But I've been out a year. Trying to get my kids back. But they're so attached to Shirley now."

Shirley stepped in. "You can have your younger children back as soon as the court gives them back to you. Have I ever denied you any visits?" Shirley didn't mention that Chica had adopted Trayvon and Malibu. She was the foster parent to the younger three, though.

"True dat, Mami. I love you for all you've done for the kids." Then she turned to me and showed me the smallest diamond ring I'd ever seen. "But the good news is I'm getting married."

"Yeah?" I was shocked. Who would want to marry a woman with five children with almost that many daddies? But you never knew.

"Yeah, to a Riley Whitmore. We met in rehab eight months ago, and although they say you're not supposed to have a relationship for the first two years, we fell in love. We tried not to get serious for a year, and we just couldn't fight it any more."

"What?" I didn't say anything. I thought about my new take on love.

Love? What a joke. I hadn't dated seriously in a couple of years. I had an on-again, off-again relationship with a fellow police officer, Flag, who worked undercover in Vice out of 77th Division, but he was nothing more than a booty-call to me. After one bad marriage, and one bad living-together arrangement, I no longer even believed love was a possibility. I never wanted to live with another man, let alone deal with a man for something other than sex, and I could do that without cohabitation.

"Well, I've got to go out and let the kids see you. They say you can't have but so many people in here at a time."

After Chica left, Trayvon and Malibu came in to see me. They were wearing back packs, like they were coming from school. Beforehand, Shirley had decided that seeing me would be too much for Soledad, Charisma, and Brooklyn so they were at home with Chill.

"Hi, Aunt Z," Trayvon leaned down and kissed me on the cheek. "We're praying for you." Trayvon, who was also my godchild, wore a curly afro, which resembled my short hair cut. He was about my height now and, even with his spread of pimples across the bridge of his nose, was becoming handsome. Whenever I took him places, people asked if he were my son.

Malibu, who was tall for twelve, handed me a single rose she'd taken out of Shirley's garden. "Love you, Auntie Z." She was already a stunning beauty, with the same long hair that Chica used to sport. Only her hair was black and had more of a wave to it, probably due to her black father.

When everyone left, I dozed back off for I don't know how long since they were keeping me doped up on Demerol, but a strangely familiar male voice startled me awake. There was an amused tone in the speaker's words.

"Hey, is this that feisty girl who ran off a gang of boys?"

I gazed up at a familiar Hispanic face, but I didn't recognize him. All I knew is that he was wearing a detective's badge, and was dressed in a suit. Then I noticed his badge. "Detective Romero."

"Do I know you?" I asked, puzzled. He seemed to act as if he knew me.

"Do you remember me? Romero Gonzalez? When I read your bio on the computer and saw your picture, I said, I think that's the girl I gave the ride that day. You haven't aged that much."

I scoffed, "Flattery will get you no where," but I felt myself smiling. By me not having children, I guess I hadn't aged as much as my friends.

"Besides, I knew there couldn't be many Zipporah's around."

I perked up and pushed the button to set my bed in a sitting position. I reached out my fist for a pound. "I don't think I ever got a chance to thank you." He gave me a pound back.

"No problem. I just hate we lost touch. I tried to call you and could never find you. I still chuckle about how you scared those knuckleheads that day."

"Did you hear what I said to them?"

"Never forgot it."

"Believe it or not, I was still a virgin at the time."

"You know I kind of figured that. There was something streetwise, yet innocent about you."

"Oh yeah?" I tried to envision my earlier eighteen-year-old self. Mmm. I guess God did look out for fools and babies.

"I'm glad getting gang raped didn't turn out to be your first time."

A memory of my first time at nineteen, which wasn't anything to write home about, crossed my mind, but at least it was consensual. Thinking of what could have happened, I commented, "I'm glad you stepped in."

"Well, you kind of had the situation under control."

I looked closer at Romero and noticed that the old tattoo on his neck had been faded as if he tried to have it removed. He was wearing an Armani suit and seemed like a different person than the man I met years ago. I guess we all had changed. I knew a lot of people who'd gotten their tattoos removed as they worked their way up into mainstream society.

"Where have you been all these years?" he asked.

I thought about it. "In L.A."

"I thought we'd keep in touch. I tried to call you, then your number got changed."

"Well, just say life got in the way. Besides, after I got on the force, I got married in Vegas, had that one annulled, married, and divorced again." I paused. "How 'bout you? Married?"

"No, I'm divorced."

"One of the job hazards, I guess."

Romero nodded, ruefully.

"It's something I wanted to ask you when we met," I said. I was thinking back to how Romero had probably been a gangbanger when he was young. I remembered the fear he inspired in my would-be attackers. And I wondered why.

"Shoot."

"What made you want to get on the force?"

"I wanted to make a difference." Romero's voice sounded earnest.

I studied him. He was really serious. I had started out with those lofty aspirations, too, but it had just become a job as time rolled by. A job which required more and more drinking for me to dull my senses.

Romero continued. "I didn't want to be another statistic. Too many of my homeboys had been killed, and I wanted to be able to turn as many lives around as I could."

I didn't comment. "What division do you work in?"

"Pacific."

Okay. So that is West Los Angeles. "Which unit?"

"Detective."

I switched gears and jumped to what was on my mind. "Do you know why someone would shoot my partner?"

"That was a known drug house. The perp had two strikes. Do the math."

I figured that Unca Pookie's house was a crack house, but after that shoot out, and being unconscious for a couple of days, I guess I'd forgotten.

"Do they have the shooter?"

"We have a Lawrence Mitchell in custody. He's denying doing the shooting though. But we found a .350 Magnum in his house. Okamoto was hit by a .350 Magnum."

From what Romero told me, Uncle Pookie was a small, low-level drug dealer. "What we found on him was enough crack to send him back to prison for life.

I guess he freaked out and started shooting. He didn't want to go back to prison the rest of his life so he went for broke. Now he's facing murder of a police officer. I hope they gas him."

After Romero left, a parade of Internal Affairs officers trailed into my room to interview me. I told the same story over and over about the shooting—that is, what I could remember, then I dozed off in a nice drug-induced sleep. I used "exigent circumstances" as the reason for us not getting a warrant at Elizabeth Black's apartment, and for us taking the children to Uncle Pookie's house as a possible placement.

5

I didn't get out of the hospital in time to attend Oka-moto's funeral, but I watched brief clips of it on the news. At least he didn't leave behind a widow or small children, I thought, since he was divorced without children. Still I felt bad that I didn't make Okamoto's funeral. The media was having a field day.

As they launched the twenty-one gun salute, the guilt pierced my heart with each shot. I wept at the sight of his flag-draped coffin.

"Ashes to ashes, dust to dust," the chaplain's voice droned on.

I lay there, trying to envision my future riding in the squad car without Okamoto. Who would they give me as a new partner?

Okamoto, had been a drinker, which was how we'd become so tight. Many off days we spent barbecuing at his home in La Puente on his hibachi grill and getting wasted from morning until we passed out. Sometimes we'd be so drunk we'd have to spend the night with each other. We'd never been lovers though. We were just the best of friends. We'd both gone through our divorces together, so that had become our bond—the job, talking shit about our stupid exes and street adventures, and getting totally shit-faced. I really had every intention of going back on the streets as I sat there, the words of the Chaplain seeping into my consciousness.

My mind drifted back to our last night together. What was Okamoto going to tell me that night when we got off? I guess that was just one of those things I would never know.

I got sick of watching the news, so I changed the channel.

Meantime, everyone from the captain to foot patrol officers came to visit me and offer condolences over my five-day stay in the hospital. Funny thing was I knew something was wrong when Internal Affairs showed up. No one was speaking to me or looking directly in my eyes. They were talking at me. Yes, something was definitely up. My stomach started churning like it did whenever I sensed trouble.

When the sergeant handed me a trial board review notice, at first I didn't think anything of it. I had five in the past five years—all of them drinking-related misconduct issues. I was warned twice, and had to go to AA. I had three suspensions in the past three years, but I was still on the streets.

But as I scanned it, I read between the lines. People blamed me for Okamoto's death. They said if I hadn't been drinking I would have been more alert. But no one knew how badly I felt inside. No one had beaten themselves up more than I had. If I hadn't been drinking, then my reactions would have been better. No, no. I couldn't do anything better than I did. How were we to know that Lawrence Mitchell would turn sniper?

My head told me I did everything I could do, but in my heart, I felt as if Okamoto's death was my fault.

Due to the Rampart Division Scandals and the Community Resources Against Street Hoodlums (CRASH

Unit) debacle, now they kept a computerized track of officer misbehavior and misconduct. I was screwed.

Three weeks later, accompanied by the union rep, James Pinckert—which was a big joke since in my gut I knew beforehand he couldn't change my fate at this Board of Rights Review since he'd gotten me off before— I listened to my sentence.

The Parole Review Board consisted of seven members sitting on chairs at a long table. They represented all races, white, black, Latino, and Asian, so I couldn't exactly say I had a kangaroo court here. I sat across from them in a chair, next to my union rep.

I smelled a strange odor. The smell of the room was one of disgrace. The detectives on the case, Internal Affairs, the lieutenant, everyone was present and they were looking at me as pariah. I was no longer part of the brotherhood. I was an outsider.

"Zipporah Saldano, you have been suspended three times for drinking-related incidences, both on duty and off-duty in the past four years. The Board finds reasonable cause for termination from the Los Angeles Police Department."

Termination! What a penalty! I sat there, numb, as they took away my badge and my city-issued Beretta. The only thing I had left were my uniforms, which I bought, and cleaned out of their city allowance. I didn't have the uniform I was wearing when I got shot because they had it in evidence locked up. I was stripped to the core.

Over the past ten years, so much of my identity had been tied up with being a police officer, I didn't know what I was going to do. How would I live? My rent in the Venice Canal area was $3,000 per month. I had about 10k in the bank. Hmmm. This would be interesting.

As I was being sentenced, the only thing I could think was how funny it was that the children of alcoholics find each other. My mother and all her men had been heavy drinkers. My ex-husband, Rafael, another cop, had been a rip-roaring drunk off-duty, whom I had infamous brawls with. We had to break up before we shot each other, because, when we'd drink together, we would pull our guns on each other in a heartbeat. And Okamoto had also been a functional alcoholic.

As I sat there, frozen in my seat, I could see my future going up like a wisp of smoke from a crack pipe as they read out the sentence. What was I going to do if I couldn't identify myself as an L.A.P.D. officer? I was so stunned that I didn't even hear the union when they said they could appeal the decision. I'd been suspended before, but this was the first time I was terminated. I was too disheartened to worry about anything. I didn't know what I was going to do.

"Is this what I get for ten years of service?" I demanded when they asked me if I had anything to say.

"Well, what did you expect?" Captain Finney asked. "We tested your blood alcohol and it was .10. The public was demanding some type of action. You've been given chance after chance with this drinking. We've put you in programs, and you still keep relapsing.

"We recommend you go to an in-patient alcoholic's program, and support that with on-going AA meetings," were the last words I heard.

I didn't know how I made it home that afternoon, but all I knew was I couldn't wait to get home so I could get into my kitchen cabinet and pour another drink. *How did I get caught up in so much scandal and wrongdoing?* I wondered.

I lost my job as a police officer. I was blamed by all my fellow officers for Okamoto's death. The media was having a field day with my downfall and had gone on a smear campaign to ruin my reputation—or what was left of it. It was open season on misconduct of L.A.P.D.

No one remembered I was once a decorated cop for bravery in the face of a sniper. All they knew was I had fucked up, my partner was dead, and someone had to be blamed. Although I didn't go to jail, I became a prisoner by my addiction. I took a drink on the night of a case that was to become a media fiasco.

Six weeks later, after I was released from my doctor's care for the bullet wound, I began to drink so much I lost track of how much I was drinking. I'd drink first thing in the morning and before going to bed. I couldn't stop. I don't know if I ate. I just know for nine months I was lost in a bottle.

Although I told my union rep I was going to seek help for my addiction, I didn't. The truth was I really didn't mean it, but as part of my trial board I was advised to go to AA meetings. I hadn't been to one meeting and I'd been drinking ever since I was fired.

I was also advised to see a therapist, and I did see the city shrink a couple of times for my resulting "post traumatic stress disorder", but I never opened up and told the truth so it didn't help. The only thing that seemed to help was to drink. It became a vicious cycle. I drank so I didn't remember and as a result, I didn't know how or if my bills got paid.

Apparently I didn't pay them, because suddenly lights were cut off, the phone was cut off and the gas was cut off. The only reason the water was on was that the co-op paid it. It was too much to even believe that this could happen to one person.

I felt guilty because I never rescued my younger brother and sister out of the foster care system, and I felt guilty because I was the one who caused our family to be split up. My father was dead and my mother was locked up because of what I did. I'd lost touch with my oldest brother after joining the police force. What was I to do?

I decided that I would get a job, but for the first time I glanced in a mirror. I looked God awful. My bobbed hair was standing all over my head, my eyes looked like how I imagined scarlet fever would make your eyes look, and I was so dehydrated I felt like a hot box had set up residency in my chest. I didn't know what to do with myself. I decided then I needed help.

I picked up a phone book and called Alcoholics Anonymous, but I ended up taking another drink and forgetting about that plan. These words remained engraved in my head.

On 12-31-06, at approximately 04:00 hours after your partner's death in the line of duty, you were found to have 0.10 alcohol content in your system, which rendered you incapable of backing up your partner.

6

I woke up in a cold sweat, twisting and turning from my recurring nightmare. This dream came every so often and it reminded me of the Temptations' song because I kept having the same one about "the day my daddy died."

In the nightmare, after my father got shot, he sat up, bullet hole in his chest, and said to me, "Wake up, Zipporah. I can't save you now. You have to save yourself."

I fought to pull myself out of the jaws of this dream. As I slowly drifted back into consciousness, I felt an erection poking in my back. Its owner, my "friend," Officer Gerald Tyler, known as Flag by everyone in the department, was spooning me.

"Come on, baby, give me some more."

I blinked to clear my eyes. Everything appeared watery. I saw my candles burning throughout the room and flickering on the wall since my lights were currently still cut off. As my room came into focus, I noticed everything seemed turned upside down. Did I do this while I was under the influence? But my mind was on what Flag had said.

I turned and glared at this fool. No he didn't say 'some more?' Did I have sex with him?

I never fooled myself into thinking I loved Flag, but he was, and still is, bar none, the best lover I ever had. At the same time, I never deluded myself about him though. He was a male whore, using his badge to get all the women he could, which is why he couldn't stay married. To my knowledge, he'd been divorced three times. But Flag—also known as 'the Flagpole' in the bedroom—knew he could give out some thug-lovin'.

I understood Flag grew up in Compton. As a narcotics undercover cop, I often wondered which side of the law he was on, he dressed so street. Sagging pants. The whole bit. I also kept promising myself I would stop messing with him before he caused me to have a complete hysterectomy, but his loving was like crack. You had to ease off it—you couldn't just go cold turkey, and hit it and quit it.

Anyhow, I vaguely remembered Flag coming over last night, but I'd gotten so wasted I couldn't remember us having sex. He was actually an ex-boyfriend later relegated to a booty-call, so I don't know what he was doing in my bed. I turned around, looked down and saw his naked penis bobbing up towards my hips.

"Where's your condom? Did you use one last night?"

I groaned inside. I was going to have to stop all this drinking. Flag was just too promiscuous to not use a condom with. It would be like playing a game of Russian roulette with my life. No way was he running up in me raw. Or did he?

"Yeah, I had a bag on old boy, here." He glanced down at his manhood, poking out his chest. He was proud of his length and his girth. He was truly hung, but unfortunately, his penis was attached to an idiot—a good looking one at that. Although he was black, people thought that Flag was Chicano or Dominican or something because of his wavy black hair and apricot complexion.

"Show it to me." I was adamant, even if I was still semi-drunk.

He reached in the small waste paper basket I kept by my bed and pulled up a used condom filled with sperm.

"Good." I looked around my ransacked room. The drawers were turned over and clothes were strewn all over the floor. *Did I do this while I was drunk?* I wondered again. I really did need to quit all this drinking. Perhaps I would go to rehab. Then it hit me. What if Flag did this? What was he looking for?

"Hey, what the hell happened to my room?" I asked. "Did you do this?"

Flag gave me a blank look. "I dunno. It was like this when I got here. What the hell you been doing around here?"

I shrugged, then reached beneath my bed and pulled out a short dog. I sucked in a deep swig and I let out a satisfied "Ahhhh!"

"You need to lay off that shit, Z," Flag said, reaching for my half-pint bottle.

Only a person who was in my shoes could understand how I felt. When I used to see the drunks on the corner and in the park, I used to think they were weak. That's how they got there. But now I understood how they got there. Life kicked them in the ass and brought them to their knees. Now people looked at me with disgust, but unless you were hurting, like I was hurting, you couldn't judge a person. I was not weak. I just couldn't take any more.

I slapped his hand away. "Leave my shit alone."

Flag's tone turned serious. "I know you and Okamoto were close, but you've got to pull yourself together."

"Yeah, we were close."

"Did he ever tell you anything about what he was going to Internal Affairs for?"

"No. Why you want to know?" I turned and looked at him suspiciously.

"Oh, I was just wondering." Flag waved his hand in dismissal.

I gulped down another deep swallow and let out an exaggerated belch. "Oops, excuse me." I covered my lips. The truth was, I was in a space where I didn't give a flip for or about social proprieties.

"Com'on, Z, put that bottle down."

"Go screw yourself, Flag."

"No, I wanna screw you." He placed his finger on the side of his nose as if he was pondering something. "Girl, you know your bullet hole scar is sexy." Flag began tracing my scar from my surgery and the hole where the bullet came out through my upper back shoulder.

"You're so ghetto." I chuckled softly and felt myself weakening, but I forced myself to slip on my night shirt which was crumpled at the foot of the bed. I was determined not to give in.

Obviously, the word about my termination had traveled around the station and the other divisions like gossip on the underground railroad. Being a police officer had its own little subculture, so why not? I even received a few phone messages on my answering machine. "Z, I heard about that shit that went down. Are you going to fight back? Pull the race card on they ass."

"Yeah," I'd say out loud to my answering machine. "I'ma fight this shit." The truth was I'd think about appealing the decision, but then I'd go get drunk instead. I was too guilt-ridden over Okamoto's murder to fight for my old job. I just couldn't face working as a police officer again.

Anyhow, since my divorce, Flag and I had been on-again, off-again lovers now for the past three years. Good sex was really hard to find these days was the excuse I gave myself—so many men in their thirties were already using Viagra, but I really was trying to wean myself off this man.

"I've got to get out of here," I announced, dangling my legs over the bed.

"What's the matter?"

"I've got to go pick up my mother today."

"Oh, so she's getting out?"

"Yeah. They transferred her down to County, so I just need to help her get to a halfway house."

For years my mother had been incarcerated in Central California Women's Facility. Last week, her parole officer had contacted Shirley, who, in turn, called me. When I said I wasn't going to pick Venita up, Shirley got on me. "She is your mother," she said pointedly. "The Bible says to honor your mother and father so that it will go well with you. It's always better to do the right thing."

"I don't owe her anything," I said through gritted teeth. I fumed over the idea for a few days, but in one of my rare moments of hung-over sobriety, I decided I'd go pick Venita up on today's date. I wanted to confront the woman who was the cause of all my present day problems. I guess that was why I started drinking yesterday before Flag showed up.

"I thought you didn't even keep up with her," Flag said, interrupting my reverie.

"What kind of hold does your mother have on you?"

"Hey, that's my moms you're talking about." I switched gears on him. "How did you get in here?" I asked, still trying to remember letting him in. I knew I was drunk, but how did I let this fool in?

He reached his hand out to me. "You're kidding, aren't you?"

I decided to pretend I remembered letting him in. "Hey, I'm just playing."

Flag reached his hand out to mine. "Come with me and be my love. Who is that, baby?" As part of the package, Flag also quoted love poetry, which felt like an oxymoron for his thugged-out appearance, but it was also part of his quirky appeal. He made me think of Jada Pinkett and Allen Payne in the movie *Jason's Lyric*.

"John Donne. But that's not what I asked you." I stuck to the point.

"I thought you said we could get back together last night."

"No, I didn't." Now I knew I had to stop this drinking.

"Com'on. Let's just do it one more time for old time's sake. We did it last night."

"I don't think so. When I'm through I'm through. You cooked your own goose." I was trying to remember the wrong he'd done when we were dating, but I'd forgotten. I knew it was some other woman—too many to even bother fighting over. He wasn't the most discreet player.

"Okay. Your loss." He climbed out of the bed, circling his member in his hand, trying to entice me.

The truth was I hadn't forgotten how good the sex was. It was just the empty feeling I couldn't stand afterwards. Anyhow, he said we did it when I was drunk last night. I didn't even remember it.

Before I could throw Flag out, I heard this loud rapping at my door and it made me jack knife out the bed. I stumbled onto the slate marble floor, still half high, kicking clothes out of my path, and staggered out the room. I passed through my open floor plan that boasted a loft on the second floor, then bounded down the stairs, holding the pinewood stair rail, head splitting in half from my hang over. I flung open the door, shouting, "Who is it?"

And there stood Romero. "What are you doing here?" I asked, my hand on my hip.

"I thought you might could use a friend."

"Oh, so who sent you?"

"Nobody. I came as a friend."

"Friend? I don't know you. Stay away from me. I don't need a good Samaritan now. I'm a grown woman." As far as I was concerned, he was throwing salt in my game. He didn't have any business coming by unannounced. Maybe I was about to take care of business. He didn't know that.

I slammed the door in his face, but I felt funny, seeing Romero's hurt expression.

I peeked through the stained glass window in my oak door and watched him stride up the sidewalk along the man-made canal. I loved the canal. I loved my clapboard two-story house, and I loved the ocean view from my window. I often walked down to Venice Beach from my condo.

It was after Romero disappeared that I noticed a card he shoved under the door. It read the House of the Future Rehab. *I don't need no rehab*, I thought. What was he talking about? I stuck it in my jacket pocket, which was hanging on a coat tree in my foyer. Suddenly, I noticed my console cabinet doors in my living room were open and papers were scattered all over the floor. Damn. Why did I trash my house like this? I scratched my head. What was I looking for? I couldn't even remember. Lord, I really needed to quit all this drinking. After today, I was going to quit.

I went and picked the papers up off the floor. As I stood up, I caught a glimpse of myself in the gilded wall mirror. I looked a hot mess. My hair stood on end like a Senegalese jungle, and in a moment of clarity, I saw myself through Romero's eyes. I *did* look like a drunk.

I climbed the stairs back to the bedroom, in time to see Flag hanging up his cell phone.

"Who was that at the door?" Flag asked, regarding who was at the front door.

I didn't answer. "Who was that on the phone?"

"That was Anderson, my partner." A stricken look, almost one of apprehension, flitted across his face.

"What did he want?"

"He just wanted to know if we were going to the Laker's game this weekend."

I knew he had a white partner named Julius Anderson and they had been partners for a long time, but I didn't believe that was Anderson on the other line. Even so, I ignored Flag's lie and, out of a sense of perverseness, or maybe a sense of rebellion against Romero trying to run my life, I decided to let Flag finish what he started. I wanted to forget the mess I made of my house. I wanted to escape the fact I couldn't even remember trashing my own place.

"Let's take a shower," I cooed, pulling him toward my large marbled bathroom with the ten by twelve granite shower. In addition to the foreplay, I knew a good shower would sober me up.

"Let's play police and prostitute," Flag whispered in my ear as he soaped my back side. "Hook me and book me, baby."

"It's on," I murmured.

And freaky as Flag was, liking S&M, loving me to use handcuffs on him since I played the officer, and he the male prostitute, I complied. When we stumbled out the shower into the bedroom, I pulled out my police belt. He liked me to flog his buttocks with my belt, and at least, this time I was not as drunk anymore—I was only hung over—so, when we finally got busy, I reached a good climax, which should tide me over for a while, I hoped. I promised myself that I was through with Flag. But I saw him again and again after that. He was like drinking alcohol for me—an irresistible drug.

A couple of hours later, I whipped off the Hollywood Freeway into northern downtown. I hadn't seen my mother since I was nine, so I would never have recognized her when she came through the County Jail's gates at Bauchet Street at North Vignes Street.

Over the years, Shirley had been communicating with my mother, and she was the liaison person who received all the original letters to me. I guess I still had Shirley on my contact information as next-of-kin, and the parole board had her contact me earlier last year, then again last week.

"Zipporah," a strange voice called out to me. "It's your mother."

I looked up to see a slattern looking strange woman. Venita? Was that my mother Venita? In my memory, she'd never aged. She was still in her early twenties, which was the last age I saw her.

I couldn't believe how haggard she looked now. She had come out of prison looking like somebody's death warmed over. The big breasts and big behind that she'd been famous for in the projects was gone. She was all angles. She was wearing her once beautiful long hair cut close to her scalp.

Just say Venita had not aged well. At fifty, her hair was gray, and she had no teeth. I couldn't believe it. She used to be a showstopper of a woman. My God, what happened to her?

"Zipporah?" she said, staring at me. I guess she still remembered me and, from pictures provided by Shirley, knew how I looked twenty-three years later.

She hugged me, and I just stood with my arms hanging to my side. Does this woman know how much destruction she has wrought in my life and those of my siblings? Why did she have to be a Crip? Why couldn't she have been a normal mother, whatever that was?

"Hi." I flashed her a fake smile.

"Are you all right? Shirley told me what happened to you."

"I'm fine." My voice sounded cold even to myself.

"So good to see you. Did you get my letters?"

"No. I didn't get them." I think about all the letters I refused to open or had burnt that Shirley had given me. I blamed her for my father's death. If she hadn't been who she was, he would have never gotten killed, as far as I was concerned. I don't even see how my father got involved with her anyhow. He was a UPS driver, and a law abiding citizen. She was too wild for his lifestyle, but he made sure he picked me up every weekend up until the day he died.

We were silent on the drive as I took the Santa Monica Freeway West to Crenshaw Ramp exit. I drove her over to a courtyard of a four-family flat on Crenshaw. This was one of the many sober living and half-way houses peppered all around L.A.

"Do you know where David is?" Venita asked when we pulled up in front of the address she'd given me to drop her off.

I almost snapped, "Who?" and then I remembered Mayhem's birth name was David. Ironically, my mother named us all out of the Bible. David, Zipporah, Daniel, and Righteousness. I never remembered her taking us to church, but apparently, she knew her Bible.

I sucked my teeth in disgust. "Still banging with his old self. Selling drugs. In and out of prison. I'm not sure if he's in or out now."

"You have his number?"

"No. Why?"

"He is your brother. Why not? You used to idolize him when you were a little girl. You used to follow him around all day and say, 'Who, Dave, Mama?'"

I hated to cut Venita's stroll down memory lane short, but she made me want to puke. "Do you know where Righteousness and Diggity are?"

She gasped, as if I hit her in her Adam's apple. "No." Her voice sounded humble and penitent.

"They were both adopted, as far as I know," I went on. "Anyhow, I was never able to get them like I thought I would when I got grown." I turned and hardened my face, angry at her for my failing. I was silent as we pulled off into the traffic.

Venita finally broke the silence. "Why are you so angry at me?"

I kept my eyes on the road as I spoke in a voice which almost sounded like a demon; it was so filled with hate. "Venita, you were just so weak for men. It's bad enough you were out there banging when we were kids, but none of this would have happened had you not been so dick-happy."

Venita sucked in her breath, as if I slapped her. "Oh, so now you're grown so you can talk any kind of way to your poor mother. . . . That hurts, but I guess I deserve it."

I was on a roll though, fueled by years of frustration, abandonment, and rage, and I continued. "You killed my father."

"You know I didn't kill your father. I tried to help him."

"But that's why he's dead."

Venita was quiet for a while. When she spoke, her words were measured. "Zipporah, we get no do-overs

in this life," she said. "But I'd appreciate it if you remember I am your mother. I did give birth to you—not
you to me—okay?"

We both shut up. *Mother. Hah! What a joke! You
weren't there for me in the years I lived with you, so busy
gang banging or running with your men, let alone after
you went to prison.*

Years of silence fell between us, creating a wall that
neither one of us wanted to climb over. Neither one
of us wanted to go back and revisit that life-changing
night.

When she got out my car, we didn't even say good-
bye. I helped her carry her little duffle bag to the front
door, then walked back and climbed in my car and
headed home so I could get drunk again.

7

AA Step 1. *We admitted we were powerless over alcohol—that our lives had become unmanageable.*
It was almost nine months after I got fired before I completely sobered up. I guess I hit bottom when I went to a bar on Alameda, had a black out, and didn't wake up until three days later in McArthur Park. I was laying on a park bench when I came to. I looked around and then had my last recollection of sharing a bottle of wine with a bum in the park. I felt all over my body to see if I'd been violated, but I didn't feel any evidence of it. I had no idea where my car was, so with the few dollars I had in my pocket, I caught the public bus home.

But, it got worse. I stumbled home to find my furniture sitting in the driveway and on my lawn like some tent city under the freeways here in L.A. Obviously, the county sheriff had put me out. A padlock was on my door. I hadn't paid rent since I was fired. Even though I drew down my pension, I blew most of the money while I was blacked out on benders. Not knowing what to do, I did what I did best. I trudged to a local liquor store and copped another bottle of Hennessy with the last twenty I found in my pants pocket. I came back and sat on my front porch, sipping and trying to figure out what I'd do next.

I didn't know how and where Shirley came from, but she was standing over me when I passed out on my front yard. Maybe the neighbors had called her.

"You're not coming home until you dry out," I remembered Shirley saying, as she lifted me up and placed me in her car.

Shirley, the collector of abandoned children and stray dogs, took me in—once again—took me by the hand, bathed me, cleaned me up, sat through a week of one of the world's worse detox in history, accompanied by chills, tremors, sweats, dry heaves, hallucinations, and then, finally, the runs. After a week, Shirley finally got some food down in me that would take hold in my stomach. When she felt I was strong enough, she took me by the hand, once more, then put me in the twenty-eight-day detoxification program that Romero left the card for that was still in my jacket. The program in San Pedro was called House of the Future and it was a turning point in my life.

House of the Future was located down by the Pacific Ocean in San Pedro. From the second-story floor, which had an outside veranda along the back, you could both see and smell the ocean, which gave the residents a soothing feel. This was a place you could see yourself getting sober in. The refurbished Victorian home possessed an old rustic feel. Walnut-stained hardwood floors, a library in the front room filled with some of the great philosophers of our times, wood cane back chairs, which made you think you were in an antique museum. Clusters of tiger lilies, begonias, impatiens, geraniums, and bougainvillea filled the front yard. A few stray tomcats hung around, waiting to be fed by the residents. The house was wrapped around by a white picket fence, which drew up childhood memories of my father's bungalow in Compton.

***

That first afternoon, as I headed to my bedroom, I was thinking how I hated sharing my personal space with someone I didn't know. I really didn't like the idea that I was going to have a roommate. I was advised my roommate was named Haviland and I'd seen her when we were at the first orientation meeting. She appeared to be about in her early thirties, and had a young, well-cared for pampered appearance about herself.

As I sauntered into my assigned room and witnessed my new roommate, Haviland, having a melt down on her cell phone, I was shocked.

"Mother, I know you're there. The gig is up! You know I need this money. Daddy left that money to me. Bitch, give me my money!"

I stared on in amazement at how out-of-control Haviland was acting. She was wearing designer clothes, had Prada, Gucci, Fendi, and Coach bags on lockdown from what I could see on her shelf, so I didn't know why she was acting like she was some broke ass chick.

I was still shocked to hear someone talk to their mother like that though. Growing up, and other than when I spoke up to Venita the day she got out of jail, if I'd ever talked like that to my crazy birth mother, or even to my foster mother, Shirley, I'd be needing teeth implants.

I could still hear Venita's voice bellowing throughout our projects whenever we messed up. "I'll smack the taste out your mouth and knock your ass into next week."

Or the smooth way Moochie would get you back since she was under the DCFS supervision. "Call the child abuse hotline if you want to, but I'm the queen of this house. I'll be waiting at the door for them. Where you gon' be?" And it always worked, because no one ever wanted to be moved from Shirley's home. We'd all read the horror stories in the *L.A. Times* of what could happen in the luck-of-the-draw type of foster homes you could land up in.

Finally, she spoke to me. "Hey, name's Haviland."

"Yes, I met you at orientation. My name is Zipporah."

"Z, is it all right if I call you Z?" She lit up a cigarette.

I nodded in the affirmative. "That's what everyone calls me."

"I understand you're a cop."

The counselor had introduced me as a cop to the group. "Not anymore."

"But don't you know how to find things?"

"Like what?"

"Actually more like people. I'd like you to find my birth mother and birth father to see if there's any money there."

"Whoa, slow down. Why are you so money hungry?"

"Look, I deserve this money," Haviland snapped. "These white people adopted me. I gave them their little fantasy about having a baby. Now they owe me. And my birth parents owe me, too."

"Why do you think your birth parents owe you money?"

"For giving me away like garbage."

I shook my head. Just listening to her talk was like listening to a rake going over a glass driveway, her speech was so abrasive and nonsensical. "Can't say you don't have issues, can we? But the truth is, I don't have the same access to information now that I'm no longer an officer."

"Why not? Don't you have connections who could help you?"

"Not for this."

"To tell you the truth, I'm in a jam."

"Oh." I decided not to probe.

Haviland continued. "For the past three months, since my adoptive father died and since the reading of the will, I've been speaking into an answer machine. I've tried blocking out my number and she still won't answer. I know the Bible says, 'Honor thy mother and father,' but how could Mom do this to me? The Bible didn't say anything about the parents messing over the kids."

"How did she mess over you?"

"I was her baby, even if she didn't carry me inside of her. Doesn't she know, it's not my fault how I feel. I can't help feeling like she's abandoning me. My mother has even gotten a restraining order against me where I can't go on their estate in Beverly Hills."

"Well, have you given her any reason to think that you might harm her?" I asked.

Haviland shook her hand. "No, it seems like once people know you've had a substance abuse or alcohol problem, they always look at you like you some freakin' crack head. I was only into prescription drugs. The doctor prescribed them for me. I wasn't on no crack, but you wouldn't believe it the way this bitch who adopted me is acting." Havilland kicked her Louis Vuitton suitcase across the room.

"Don't you think your mother might have a reason to be afraid of you?" I asked, seeing how wild and violent she was acting.

"Let me explain my situation. My therapist says I have abandonment issues. Me and my boyfriend were facing foreclosure big time in our Hollywood Hills house—who isn't right now? But that's not the point. I had money due me, that's what makes me so mad. My father meant for me to have that money. She's lying when she said my father wrote me out the will and the trust. Anyhow, me and my boyfriend got robbed at gunpoint during a home invasion right after I cashed my check when I did get my royalties, so that's why I lost my money ." She looked down at her wrists, pulled up her long sleeved blouse, and revealed bandages on both arms.

I started to ask her what happened to her wrists, but I knew a suicide attempt when I saw one. She was definitely a certified nutjob.

So this was how and where I met my roommate, Haviland McIntire, former child star, current Vicodin queen. I found out that Haviland had been adopted as an infant by a white couple back in the '70s, when interracial adoption was uncommon. Although she was African American, she said her birth mother was white and her birth father was black. She looked like a light-skinned black girl, but her roan-colored hair was bone straight.

Thinking back, I vaguely remembered seeing Haviland playing in an eighties TV sitcom called *We Are One World*. She was on the show from about age eight to thirteen when the show was really popular. Her face graced all types of teen magazines and she even went on Oprah back in the day. She gained a lot of notoriety, even as a teen actress, but her drinking and drugging derailed her career. I figured that we were about the same age because I saw the show after I went into foster care and was living with Shirley.

I wondered what Haviland was doing in a drug program, but during my thirty-day stay, I saw several other celebrities. I guess there was as much pressure to remain in the spotlight for actors as there was for police officers to go to work and come home alive each day.

8

"Spiritually, we choose our parents so that we can learn the life lessons that we were sent here to learn."

That's what my sponsor, and our group leader, Joyce told us in our first meeting where everyone was blaming their parents for how 'fucked up' our own lives were. Haviland was so obnoxious during that first meeting she made me cringe in embarrassment for her. She was a repeat offender whose recidivism for drug programs obviously was up there in the double digit numbers. Perhaps that was why Joyce singled her out, saying that Haviland suffered from this syndrome called "narcissistic injury." When Haviland continued to cut up during the meeting, Joyce used the term "narcissistic rage."

During our four weeks of treatment, I experienced a range of emotions myself, which boomeranged between self-defense to self-loathing. This was also the first time I learned the idea that we must deconstruct in order to reconstruct our lives. As time passed, I really couldn't scrutinize Haviland anymore because I was going through my own melt down.

The first time I stood up at the podium at a twelve-step meeting and said, "My name is Zipporah and I'm an alcoholic," I could have died from the shame of it all—like a cartoon character reduced to a pool of ink. I wished the ground would open up and swallow me.

***

I guess I'd developed the police force mentality of being above the law. I never faced it before, but, over the ten years as an officer, I drank the Kool-Aid and believed in its superiority and self-righteousness. Just being in this program was an admission of my human frailty and vulnerability.

This place was breaking me down in ways I didn't like. My ego shattered as the group broke through all my defense mechanisms. I would get livid when these strangers would get all in my face and challenge the lies I had told myself.

"You're an alcoholic, Z," Joyce said. "You can't keep everything inside of you. You need help just like the rest of us. Open up and let someone in."

"I don't give a flip," I shouted back, then retreated into silence the rest of the group meeting.

First of all, they didn't know me. I was told this so often, I guess that was my problem. I did tend to keep everything inside of me, but I was not used to opening up with friends, let alone strangers. I started opening up just enough to keep the group off my ass.

Although I didn't share any of my crazy antics I committed while I was drunk, I finally admitted, "Drinking cost me my job. I lost my house. I lost my self-respect. Now there, y'all satisfied?"

Once they got off my case, I started noticing the people around me. That's when things got a tad bit easier for me.

There was an Emmy award-winning actor, Mike, who looked like a faded-out beach surfer. I kind of remembered him from an old TV show, *Hawaii Five-O*. He'd been a polydrug abuser. There was also an anorexic-looking, bleached-blonde meth addict named Amy—a Paris Hilton look-alike. But Haviland was the most interesting.

At a group meeting the night after I heard her go off on her mother, I listened to Haviland's testimony closer than before. She had the cynosure of all eyes as an actress, and the whole audience was held spellbound. I looked on as Haviland gesticulated all over the place like someone doing sign language. She used her hands to paint the picture.

"My name is Haviland, and I'm an addict. I used to be Hollywood's Black Flava ten years ago, but now I'm a washed-up has-been on the C-list.

"See. I was adopted at birth and raised by a white adoptive mother and father, so just say I'm a mixed nut. As you can see, I'm as brown as wheat. I'd like to blame my parents, like I tell my therapist, but the truth is, they were good to me. Paid for my two college degrees.

"Maybe, they shouldn't have adopted me. It's my adoptive parents' fault for the predicament I'm in. Why? Because they raised me to think I should only have the finer things in life. I've been called a spoiled brat by all three of my ex-husbands.

"To say I've been backsliding is an understatement with this treatment thing, but this time I'm going to really try to stay straight. I might even go back to church. Yeah, I admit I haven't been to church in many moons. I had been raised part Jewish, where I went to the synagogue with my parents, but was allowed to visit Black churches so I could stay in touch with my culture. Then, as an adult, I joined the Church of Scientology for a while.

"Anyhow, last week I got tired of it all, and I tried to end it. When I woke up in the hospital, I decided I wanted to get clean and stay that way."

Now, the more I listened to Haviland's story, the better I understood why she behaved the way she did. She *was* spoiled rotten. I didn't feel an iota of pity for her. I wished some Beverly Hills couple had adopted my ass out of Jordan Downs when I was a baby. Get over yourself. Boo hoo freakin' hoo. Get over yourself already.

A week later, when we had the group meeting where our parents or family members come to participate, since addiction is viewed as a family problem, Shirley came as my mother. Right away, I noticed Haviland did not have anyone come to fill in as her family member. I guess her mother was just too burnt out with her addiction.

Although my mother, Venita, was out of prison, I didn't invite her, because one, she was a stranger to me as far as I was concerned, and two, I didn't want her to know that I was an alcoholic. Not that she should say anything since I probably inherited the gene from her. Those first nine years I grew up watching her down forties like they were Kool-Aid and smoke weed in front of us like cigarettes. I grew up knowing the smells of marijuana and alcohol like it was our air freshener. I never knew if Venita ever used anything heavier though. I'm not sure if she'd look down on me, but I felt kind of ashamed. Particularly in light of the fact that I looked down on her all these years. Now I was the drunk in need of treatment. Ain't that a blip?

Instead, I asked Shirley to represent me as family because I knew that she'd gone through the rehab bit with Chica, and stood in as the surrogate parent. She knew about addiction, relapse, and recovery and how tenuous the whole process could be.

As soon as Shirley walked in, to my surprise, Haviland leaped out of her chair, knocking it over. She ran up to my foster mother and threw her arms around her. "Miss Shirley! What are you doing here?"

Shirley looked taken aback at first. She gave her a strange look which made me think she didn't know her. She didn't say anything. Meantime, I was too shocked to react. What was going on? I wondered.

Haviland continued, "It's Haviland. Remember my mother, Ilene Rosenthal?" Shirley's face lit up. Obviously, she recognized Haviland.

"Haviland? Is that you? Where's your mom? I haven't talked to her in a while."

"Well, you and me both. I haven't talked to her since my father died three months ago. She wouldn't even let me attend the funeral."

"I'm sorry to hear about your father. The last time I talked to your mother she told me you were just getting out of rehab and that you were back into acting."

"Well, let's just say I backslid."

The group convened once all the families got there. During this family session where just about everyone in the group had someone representing them, Haviland really acted out. She ragged on her mother, calling her a racist bitch, to the point that Shirley spoke out.

"Look, Haviland, your mother's not here to defend herself. Stop all this mommy bashing, and I'll sit in for you—if it's okay?"

Haviland looked sheepish, but I recognized the look in her eye. A look I remembered having when Shirley would show up for parent-teacher conferences while I was growing up. It was one of relief. I guess we all just wanted our mothers—or a "Big Mama" or a foster mother or someone to fill that void.

It turned out that Shirley and Haviland's adoptive mother, Ilene Rosenthal, had been friends of sort, as much as blacks and whites would befriend each other in the 70s and 80s. I never met Haviland before because Shirley only attended Foster Care Association meetings or parties alone or with Chill. She didn't want us to feel like foster children with a brand on us so she never even took us to foster care Christmas parties. She bought our Christmas and birthday gifts out of her own pocket. The rest of the county money was spent on our extracurricular activities and travel.

Apparently, Shirley had met Haviland's adoptive mother through the foster care and adoption association. I learned they both volunteered at McLaren Hall, and although Shirley had been to a function or two at Haviland's home in Beverly Hills, she'd never invited Mrs. Rosenthal to our home.

9

Shirley attended the weekly family sessions with me, and she also visited me every weekend for the first three weeks.

Although Venita said to me, "We get no do-overs," in the AA program, we're supposed to try to make amends with the people we have harmed while we were in our addiction. I didn't even know where to begin.

As part of making amends and also to get uplifted, I went to visit Shirley before I graduated from my program when I got my first and last weekend pass on my fourth week in the program.

"Shirley, I'm sorry for all the lies I told you when I was in the twelfth grade and was skipping school with Chica."

Shirley laughed. "I knew about it. I remember both of your report cards saying you'd missed seventeen days of school in your senior year. I knew I sent both of you out to school every day."

"Moochie, believe it or not, we weren't having sex. We were just hanging out, going to ditch parties."

"Well, it's a good thing y'all were even able to graduate."

We both laughed. Shirley had always said we had to finish high school, so she did get to see us cross the stage and get our high school diploma.

We wound up having a comfortable talk, our first woman-to-woman chat together. Afterwards, Shirley surprised me when she offered me the rental of her garage, which she had renovated and which was supposed to be her little art studio.

"The rent is free until you find work," Shirley said.

"For real? Thanks, but I think I've got a way to make money that will be something I'd like to do."

"What is it?"

"I'd like to become a private investigator. I have a case already—if I decide to take it."

After I told her about my plan to get my certification as a private investigator, I could tell she was pleased.

"You know, that seems to be right up your alley. You can take all your police experience and use it that way. You're my girl. I knew you'd land on your feet."

Her words of encouragement brought tears to my eyes and it built a new resolve within me. I became more determined to stay sober. Besides, I knew it would be easier to stay sober, living under Shirley's watchful eye.

I moved back in with my foster mother, and once again I was glad I had her there for me. I guess I was a part of the boomerang generation at thirty-four, and, although I didn't like it, I really didn't have another choice. I had little or no money at this point. I drank up all my pension while I was on my nine month binge. So what else could I do?

I read that here on earth, we make our own heaven and hell. I'll let you decide. Maybe I made my own hell when I was drinking. I was clean since I went into rehab, but it sure wasn't heaven. I felt uncomfortable all the time. It wasn't that I wanted another drink, it was just that I could see clearly now all the damage I did while drinking and it hurt like hell to look at it.

I started my new life, living in a garage apartment that was only about a tenth as big as my condo in Venice, yet, for the first time in a long time, I had peace of mind. My living space included a living area, a let out bed, which doubled as a futon, a small kitchen area and a half-a-bath with a shower stall. I brought my new Bible, and AA's Big Book. I decided not to buy a TV. Besides, I had my laptop, which I could download movies on if need be.

I used to love to read, but I lost my books when I was evicted. I found a used copy of Toni Morrison's *Beloved*, one of my favorites, at a garage sale to begin my new library. I also started back building my Urban Books library. I started with Carl Weber's *Big Girl* series, and Ashley & JaQuavis' *Cartel* series, Michelle McGriff's *Obsession 101* series, and Shelia Goss's *Hollywood* series.

I was stripped down to my bare essentials, yet I was swaddled in contentment—something I hadn't had since I first became an officer.

For a couple of months, I didn't have a car. During that time I learned a lot since I would catch the bus or hoof it. L.A.'s homeless had increased not only in number, but also in the types of faces you saw. Many of them looked like they had been good workers until the economy started going bad. I never noticed this demographic as much when I was driving. Now I even saw how people had made makeshift homes in the city bus stops at each curb. I couldn't sit on the bench and wait for the city bus because people had made their pallets and set up their grocery carts inside the shed.

During treatment, we were told not to embark on a serious relationship because of our own issues. Our counselors said we should get a plant or a pet to take care of and see if we could keep it alive for two years or so.

Well, after I graduated from the program and moved back in Shirley's garage, we were coming from Vegas with Shirley, I stumbled on to this abandoned, injured ferret. We'd taken the kids to Circus Circus during the last week of the Christmas holiday and my first week home. I didn't even play the slot machines since that's not my vice—only drinking. I let out a little prayer afterwards. I passed my first hurtle. I managed to do Vegas without drinking. Instead, I took in a few movies since I used to be a movie buff before drinking had become my primary source of entertainment.

Anyhow, this ferret was a mousey gray brown, looked part cat, part rat, part dog, and he reminded me of myself—a mongrel. I called him Ben, since he reminded me of the movie with the rat by the same name.

After I took him to the vet, got his wounds patched up, along with shots and instructions, I was on my own. Each day Ben survived with my haphazard care, I felt like I was getting healed. Ben liked to climb into the cabinets. He had already been trained to the litter box. At night, I put him in a cage, or else I had a hard time finding him because he could squeeze into the smallest cracks. In a crazy way, I kind of bonded to this ferret, too. I swear he began to look at me with a light of recognition in his little beady eyes.

Meantime, I was staying sober, as the old cliché says, one day at a time. I made my meetings every day, sometimes in different areas of L.A. A few days after I left the program, I received a call from Haviland on my fortieth day of sobriety. "I still want you to take my case."

"Are you sure you want to do this?" I asked Haviland when we pulled up in front of Westside Nursing Home in Torrance.

"Yes, it's now or never." Haviland pushed her shades on top of her head.

"Okay. I'll wait outside," I said.

Haviland was driving her Bentley. She had picked me up at a McDonald's near Shirley's house. I didn't want her to know where I lived because I still didn't trust her. Something about her was a little too unstable and sheisty for me.

Haviland nodded and climbed out the car. I sat there, reflecting over the past few weeks.

I shook my head at this serendipitous turn of events. Who would've ever thought the upshot of meeting Haviland would be that she'd become my first case? Haviland stayed on my back so much that I went on and started a search for her birth mother. Within a couple of weeks, I found her birth mother, Jill McIntire, through her social security records, which I got through Alice Thomas, an old friend from the crime lab, who also had access to the records at the police department. It really wasn't that difficult because Haviland went through an open adoption. Alice gave me Haviland's original birth certificate, not the amended one for her adoption. It turned out her mother had never married so she was easy to find with her original surname.

Personally, I thought Haviland was just too afraid to do the search herself because she was afraid of what she might find. She was afraid her mother would reject her. And although her birth mother didn't reject her, sadly, Haviland did find bad news.

We'd just left Haviland's elderly great-aunt Matilda, who had raised her mother, Jill. She lived in a small bungalow in Cerritos. Although she looked surprised to see that Haviland was black, she appeared genuinely happy to meet her.

"I always wondered what happened to the baby, but she would never talk about it, and she refused to let us talk about it."

When Haviland asked her great-aunt Matilda if she knew who her biological father was, the woman replied, "No. Jill never told us who the father was. We all knew, though, when you came out colored, that it had to be a Negro boy."

Over the course of our two hour visit, Matilda gave Haviland a list of her mother's siblings and their phone numbers. She also gave her a lot of pictures of Jill when she was a child and a teenager. Jill, who resembled Angelina Jolie, had been a busty brunette with full lips. As we were leaving, her great-aunt Matilda even gave Haviland a big hug.

So there we were, an hour later, at a nursing home, visiting her mother. Although her aunt didn't tell her, Haviland found out the bad news on her own at the nursing home, which turned out to be a hospice center. At fifty-two, her mother Jill was dying from AIDS. From her police record, I surmised Jill contracted the virus through intravenous drug use and unprotected sex. She'd had a number of drug arrests for heroin possession and accosting and soliciting.

When Haviland came out of the nursing home, her eyes looked like a rabbit's they were so rimmed in pink, and wet. She was too overcome to talk. I let her weep quietly for a few minutes before I spoke.

"Well?" I lifted my eyebrow.

Haviland wiped her eyes. "I'm so excited and happy that I've found her. These are happy tears. My mom explained everything. Why she couldn't keep me. She was only sixteen, and my father was black. Back then that was really taboo."

"Did she give you your father's name?"

"No. She said she didn't want to share that with me."

Unfortunately, Jill was in the last stages of AIDS, when they reunited. However, she had purchased an insurance policy years earlier when she was healthy and had named Haviland as the beneficiary, because the adoption had been open and Jill knew Haviland's given adoptive name.

Within a few weeks of Haviland meeting her mother, Jill passed away.

"Haviland, are you going to be all right?" I asked, really concerned about her losing her mother after such a short time of reunion.

"Yes, I'm fine. I'm just glad to have looked into the face of the woman who birthed me. That has helped. She's also put me in touch with her sisters and brothers so I do have aunts and uncles now that I didn't have before. My other mom has poisoned my adoptive relatives against me."

Haviland paid me five thousand dollars from the money she got from her mother's insurance, all of which I banked. Somehow, Haviland and I became quasi-friends.

At her request, I helped Haviland file a petition to revoke her adoptive father's will. I still wasn't able to get the will revoked, but it wound up tied up in probate court, since Haviland was contesting the will. Through word-of mouth from Haviland, I began to get a steady stream of customers. Haviland knew a lot of people in Hollywood and in the industry. Also I advertised on Craig's list.

Bit by bit, people started coming to me who wanted other people found, cheating husbands or wives followed—things they couldn't go to the police with, for one reason or another.

11

At the age of nine, when I first moved to Baldwin Hills, after a thirty-day stay in the horrible, now defunct child detention asylum, McLaren Hall, I felt like I'd landed on a different planet. Baldwin Hills has been called the Beverly Hills enclave for blacks. Although this community was less than twenty miles from where I had been raised in Jordan Downs, it was a whole new world. School on a regular basis. "Three hots and a cot," as they say in prison. But it was more than that. Shirley offered us kids love.

As a child, Shirley's home reminded me of what I'd seen of Hollywood on TV. From Shirley's back ceiling-to-floor picture windows, you could see the Hollywood sign and the ridge of the Santa Monica Mountains. On a clear day, when the smog was low, you could see panoramic views of the entire city and the L.A. basin. The area was characterized by hillside homes and streets with names such as "Don Luis", "Don Felipe" which graced the winding hills.

Although most of the neighbors were black, they were homeowners. Where I came from, most of the people were renters. Many of the Baldwin Hills homes boasted amenities such as in-ground outdoor swimming pools and Jacuzzis. Where I came from, the community center was the only place that had a swimming pool, and often it was shut down due to shootings.

Anyhow, Shirley's tri-level house was nestled on a hill and boasted five bedrooms. I always loved how my feet slid across her mahogany hardwood floors and marble kitchen floors. I had never had a room to myself until I moved to Shirley's. About a year later, Chica was placed in our home, and I had to share the room with her, but Chica and I clicked right away. We both had parents in prison and on drugs. I guess that's how we became best friends.

Unfortunately, over the years, things were so different for the teenagers coming up in L.A. than when I was coming up. Since we lived on the better side of town in Baldwin Hills, Chica and I always felt safe. Right at the foot of the hill, the Baldwin Village a.k.a. the Jungle had its own set of problems. It was home to the Baldwin Village Bloods and Black P. Stone Bloods.

Shortly after I moved into the garage, Trayvon came to me, looking sheepish.

"What's the matter, Tray?"

He hemmed and hawed. Finally, looking down at his gym shoe, he said, "I'm afraid to go to school, Auntie Z."

"Why?"

"They say that some Mexican gang is going to put a hit out on any black person. They don't care if it's a child. They say they're gonna shoot anyone wearing a white T-shirt."

"What?" I couldn't believe it.

"Yep. They say some Crips stole their drugs, and they are going to retaliate on anybody black. They don't care if it's a kid."

I was concerned about his safety so I gave him the usual black boy growing up in L.A. speech. "Always watch your surroundings. Don't wear red or blue.

Don't claim any gangs. If someone comes up to you asking, 'What set you from?' just say, 'I don't bang.'"

I wound up borrowing Shirley's car and giving him a ride to school. As we drove to school, Trayvon told me some of the happenings. Last May, the traditional, Cinco de Mayo celebration was marked by disturbances at several local high schools. According to Trayvon, the Latino and the black high school students were fighting right there on the school grounds. The black students said that the Hispanic students walked out on Black History month so they boycotted the Cinco de Mayo celebration and the fight was on. I knew from the news that more and more, there had been riots between the Black and Latino gangs, either on the streets or in the prison system. A lot of it was drug-related, and beefing over territory to deal.

Anyhow, after a few weeks, things seemed to settle back down and I began to breathe easy for Trayvon.

My world was finally getting a sense of order, that is, until one March afternoon when I went to the 'big' house, from my apartment and saw the 'for sale' sign sitting in the front yard. I had just starting paying rent in the past couple of months. To say I was a little perturbed was an understatement. I didn't want to move any time soon. I was just getting used to being sober, and any type of life changes could start me back to drinking. Unfortunately, Shirley had done this before when she was upset with Chill. I decided I was going to just sit down and find out what was up.

When I moseyed inside through the country kitchen door, the smell of garlic and tomatoes comforted my nostrils and brought up memories of growing up in these walls. I smelled my favorite meal—Shirley's famous spaghetti, and I decided to invite myself to dinner.

I too had a vested interest in what went on around here.

"Moochie, what is that 'for sale' sign doing up in the lawn—again?" I'd been through this several times in the past ten years—all these mid-life-crisis-type threatened divorces which somehow were called off just before the divorce went to court. I stood at the L-shaped kitchen island and pulled up a stool.

Shirley continued stirring her pot of spaghetti sauce. She sprinkled in handfuls of basil. This was accompanied by stir fried garlic, onion and red bell pepper. "I swear to God if California wasn't community property, I would have divorced this man a long time ago." She stopped, smacked her lips, and shook her head as if her forty-year marriage had been a waste of time.

"You don't mean that. Not all you two have gone through together."

Shirley let out a sigh. "Yes, I do. I don't care."

I thought about how I could get Shirley in a better mood. Perhaps if she thought about Chica's wedding, she'd put off the divorce and plans to sell the house. California was a community property state, and divorce could be costly. "Well, you know Chica's wedding is just a few months away." I appealed to her strong sense of family. "Com'on now, Moochie. You know she's counting on you and Daddy Chill giving her away."

Although she didn't say anything, I could see her softening. As much as Chica had stolen from Shirley while we were growing up, had given Shirley gray hairs when she was a teenager with all her running away and acting out, Shirley was the only one who went to see Chica's ass when she was in jail and in the pen. I never went—I was too wrapped up in my job as a cop. In fact, Shirley was the one who renewed her foster license and helped rear Chica's five children, and was now helping

Chica to try and get the younger three of the children back in her custody.

"Seriously, Moochie, what do you think of Riley?" I hadn't met him yet, although I saw a picture of him. He was a lanky white boy, kind of a surfer-beach boy look, who used to work in Silicon Valley. Riley used to own a dot.com before he got strung out on crystal meth. Needless to say, he'd lost everything. He was beginning to rebuild his life again too.

"He seems like a good guy . . . but—" Shirley paused before she went on.

"But what?" I interrupted.

"But, with both of them having a drug problem, I worry. Especially with her trying to get the younger kids back."

"Well, all I know is Chica must have some bad ass snatch to get a husband at this point in the game, but I sure hope she has learned that dick is not her friend."

"All right now, watch your mouth, young lady." Shirley's crisp voice reminded me of when she had Chica and me enrolled in charm school, modeling, and talent shows to build our confidence when we were teens. She never believed in impropriety or saying things that were not "lady like." Lately, I'd been working on cleaning up my potty mouth. She should have heard me whale—I mean I cursed like a sailor when I was a cop.

If anything, now that I was not around so many men, I cursed less. I decided I'd write that in on my fourth step as something I had to work on.

"No disrespect, Moochie, but I mean Chica doesn't seem to realize that men will hurt you—even the best of men. It doesn't help that she used to like all those thug types, but someone like Riley can be treacherous—with him being a recovering addict and all."

Riley, a former businessman, who was now starting back up a new online venture, surely didn't seem to be Chica's type. I guess what they said was true. Opposites attract.

Shirley looked appalled. "Z—when did you become so cynical? I know being a police officer changed you, and in some ways not for the best, but my goodness! Don't you ever want to get married again?"

I slapped my hands up and down in a "wash your hands of a matter" way. "Look, I've been married." I held my hands up in a surrender gesture. "Just say that mess doesn't work for me. I'm just not marriage material."

"I sure would love to see you settled down—"

"Hah! Everybody I know that's married is either cheating or miserable. Look at you and Chill!"

"Well, I wasn't always unhappy."

I almost asked her why she didn't sleep with Daddy Chill anymore. It made me wonder if love was meant to last a lifetime, but I decided not to go there.

"Besides," I continued, "that's how I'm making a living now. Following cheating spouses. I don't even see why Chica wants to get married."

"Well, I wish her well. But Z, you shouldn't give up on love. There's nothing like it—when it's right and when it's good."

"Yeah, yeah. If love is so grand, what happened with you and Daddy Chill?"

Shirley didn't answer and anyway, she stopped talking as Trayvon, walked in from school. Like the others, Trayvon came home with Shirley as a newborn, but he was clearly her pet. Her eyes lit up at the sight of him. "How's my boy doing?"

"G-ma. I made the Honor Roll today, so Coach can't say I won't be able to play or go to basketball camp." All the children called Shirley G-Ma for "Grandma."

I looked on as Trayvon worked Shirley's heart strings. I must admit the boy had charisma—in fact, they were all some loveable kids. I couldn't believe how they all got their start in a crack snatch, but who but God ever knows how kids will turn out?

"That's great, baby," Shirley said, as she turned the pot down to simmer.

"I have the application for basketball camp. Can you sign it?"

"After you eat. I made your favorite."

Now it was Trayvon's turn to light up. Although Chica was Chicano, Trayvon, who was biracial, looked like any medium-brown-skinned black teen. People sometimes said he even looked like he could pass for my son since he wore a curly fro about the same length as I kept my hair cropped. Like all of his siblings, Trayvon's father, Dog Bite, had been black. He'd been murdered in prison five years earlier.

Trayvon picked up a wooden ladle spoon and reached into the pot of spaghetti sauce. "Mmm, you put your foot in this spaghetti."

Shirley playfully slapped his hand. "Get out that pot, boy. Let me fix you a plate."

I remembered how I used to love me some Shirley's spaghetti, which she usually garnered with spicy Italian sausage, stewed tomatoes, bay leaf, oregano and a lot of basil when I was growing up in her home.

Within the half hour, Malibu, Soledad, Brooklyn and Charisma showed up from their nearby bus stops. They wore their backpacks attached like camel humps on their backs. They were equally excited to know this was spaghetti night, too. You would think it was steak, but I knew how it felt to have a secure meal when you might not have had one.

I joined the family for dinner, and it felt good to be part of a family again. I helped the girls set the table. We used a pussy willow from Shirley's front yard as a center piece. It was taken from one of the willow plants, which lined the yard. They stood next to a running waterfall, shaped by large rocks lined on each side that ran down the hill, as part of Shirley's landscape in the front yard. At night, the water fall lit up, something I always loved.

After we bowed our heads, Shirley led the prayer. As usual, Chill stayed in his room with his TV tray and ate while he watched TV. He'd become so reclusive the girls called him "Uncle Pete," after the demented uncle in the movie *Soul Food*.

"Auntie, are you coming to the wedding?" Trayvon asked.

"Wouldn't miss it for the world."

"I'm going to walk my mother down the aisle," Trayvon informed me.

"I'm going to be a flower girl," Brooklyn lisped.

"Good for you both." I always admired how her children loved their mama to death—even when she was all cracked out. Their loyalty was amazing.

Just peering into Chica's children's faces, I realized how I was getting older, because I could just see us sitting in those same chairs when we were the same ages as Chica's older children.

When Shirley poured a Waterford crystal stemware glass of burgundy, for a moment, my mouth watered and I felt the old familiar taste in my palate. Although she didn't offer me a drink, when I silently passed up by not asking for one, it felt good. One day at a time. I was staying sober. This was my new mantra. I could never have a social drink again. I was still struggling to accept this fact. One drink was never enough for me.

After Trayvon and the other children finished eating, he announced, "I've got a scrimmage game at Inglewood High this evening at six. Delonte's mom is going to take us."

"Do you have a ride home?" Shirley asked.

"No, ma'am. I think she's picking us back up too."

"I've got to take Malibu to drill team and Soledad to soccer so that's fine. But, call me if you need a ride."

Now that the days were longer, most of the sports were played outside on the high school field.

Trayvon turned and gazed back at me and Shirley. "Love you, G-Ma." He turned to me. "Auntie, can I wear your Starter jacket?"

I hesitated, but since it was black, I nodded. "Okay." In L.A. or Inglewood, you couldn't wear red in a Crip area, and you couldn't wear blue in a Bloods area, so Trayvon knew what time it was.

I jogged to the garage and grabbed up the vintage jacket for him. It was a perfect fit. He'd grown over the winter and was almost my height now—five feet nine.

"See you, Auntie Z. Love you."

"Love you," Shirley and I say in unison, but my mind was on something else.

"What's wrong with Daddy Chill?" I noticed he was sitting alone in the den talking to someone whom I couldn't see.

Shirley shrugged. "He's getting weirder every day. He only talks to his cockatoo, Bill." She heaved a deep sigh. "I'm just sick of living with him."

I stood at the island counter, studying my former foster mother—who was still like a mother to me. Déjà vu. It reminded me of being a child again, watching Shirley's every move. As a foster child, I learned powers of observation akin to that of a space alien. I knew intuitively when kids were going to be sent back home or replaced in another foster home. I tried to be really good so I wouldn't get replaced. I was one of the lucky ones. Shirley seldom got rid of kids unless they were unworkable like little white Tommy, the fire setter, who once burnt down the garage.

Underneath it all, though, I always felt like between Chica and me, we were kind of Shirley's favorites. There were generally two other children while we were in placement. Shirley and Daddy Chill couldn't have been better parents to us throw-away children. We had even gone on cruises with them several times while I was growing up.

I objectively examined this woman who put her fingerprints on me on the second half of my childhood. From Shirley, I learned to love nice things. Imported marble tables. Antiques. Vintage clothing, almost over designer clothing. Good art. Reading. Classical music. Shirley still drove a vintage Mustang from the 60's that was in perfect shape with its new engine and paint job.

I thought back to this pending divorce and I wondered if Shirley was going through mid-life crisis at sixty. She still had a youthful figure and appearance. Shirley couldn't even put it in words, what she was feeling, and why she wanted a divorce. From what I learned from my divorce, there was never a day of demarcation in a marriage. It was like trying to draw a line in the ocean.

Although I hadn't stayed married long, I understood where Shirley was coming from. There was never no one day where you realized you went too far, when you killed love, when somewhere along the way you stopped speaking, stopped making love, stopped loving each other. There were no bells and whistles. You just wound up on the road of no return.

Perhaps there is a season to love; a slow changing from spring, summer, winter, then back to spring. Maybe that is what happened with Shirley and Chill, I thought. They were obviously in a state of winter. Hopefully, things would thaw out and go back to spring.

This made me wonder who Shirley actually was as a woman, not just my Moochie, the woman who saved my life. I decided to change the subject, hoping that this would make Shirley forget about the divorce—for now anyhow. I didn't want any new changes in my life. I asked Shirley a question I never had considered before. "Moochie, how did you become a foster parent?"

"I had a bad relationship with my mother. I lived with my aunt the first part of my childhood, then I was sent to live with her mother when I was almost grown."

"How old were you when you went to stay with your mother?"

"I was twelve—almost grown. I never did get that closeness to her that my brother she kept with her had, though."

"Where did you live at first?"

"I grew up in the bigoted South, with an aunt who took care of me by the letter of the law, but really didn't care. Maybe that's why I became a foster mother. I can't stand to see children mistreated."

"I didn't know that."

"I always wanted to make a difference. That's why I got into the Black Panthers. That's how I met Chill. He seemed like a man who wanted to make a difference."

Her words reminded me of what Romero said to me when I was in the hospital. That he wanted his life to count, that he wanted to make a difference.

12

I shot back to my garage apartment and took a shower in my miniature half-a-bath. When I came out, I looked around the room that functioned as a living room, bedroom, and kitchen, and let out a sigh of contentment. My spot suited me just fine. A thin swath of linoleum on the back section marked off the kitchen.

Towel draped around my middle, I padded over to my IKEA desk and glanced down at the pictures I had to turn over to my latest client, a husband who suspected his wife of cheating. I perused the pile of digital photos I printed out of the wife going in and coming out the Snooty Foxx Motel on Western near Martin Luther King Boulevard. Motel Row, it was called. I was there with Flag a few years ago, and it did have the famous mirrors overhead.

Although I didn't feel good about having to give these to the husband, the job was paying eighteen hundred. At least, I was earning money again, it was legal, and like they say, "Somebody gotta do it." As an officer, I did surveillances and stakeouts before, but I didn't realize, until recently, how my police training had made me a good investigator. Last week, I bought a licensed gun—a pearl-handled Glock—but I hoped I wouldn't have to use it. I also finally purchased a used car out of the *Penny saver*.

I shook my head. *Why does anyone get married anyway? Seems like women are cheating as much as men these days, so what's the point?*

I put the pictures back in the manila envelope and slipped them into my computer's desk drawer. I could already imagine how the husband would overreact like on that show *Cheaters* when he gets the news. I cut on my laptop and checked my e-mail. I had a lot of junk mail, but I filtered through it. I put an ad for my new business, Soldano's Private Investigations, on Craig's List, and someone had already responded. Just from the wording of the email, it sounded like another husband trying to catch his wife cheating. I read a recent statistic which said wives cheated at a much higher rate than a few decades ago. I guess women's liberation had caught up in the bedroom, as well as in earning power.

Afterwards, I played with Ben as they instruct the owners of ferrets to do on the Internet, then I put him in his cage. So far, I kept him alive for several weeks, so I was doing all right. For the first time since I'd become sexually active, I admitted to myself I was not ready for a relationship. I'd been celibate for six months, if I didn't count my vibrator.

Even when Flag, as in the Flagpole, called me after I got out of rehab, and the chance at wild sex was waved in front of me like a carrot—and although my twat almost leapfrogged up in my uterus, I got so frisky just hearing his voice—somehow I found the strength to say no.

Sex and drinking often went hand in hand for me, so I had to say no. I was taking my recovery seriously this time. I stopped drinking temporarily in the past through AA meetings, but I never went to a rehab. I knew now my continued sobriety would be a matter of life or death for me. To fight down temptation, I changed my cell phone number and didn't contact Flag anymore.

Earlier that afternoon, I attended my AA meeting, which inspired me to write in my notebook. I was working on my fourth step, where I was staying stuck.

"Make a searching and fearless moral inventory of ourselves."

As I was writing out my faults, looking at my guilt regarding my younger siblings, my guilt over Okamoto's death, and my inability to forgive my mother, I decided to watch some of the old Blockbuster movies I rented.

I cut on my CD player and put on an old version of the movie, *Set it Off*. Flaws and all, I loved this movie because it featured the projects where I grew up, and the women characters were the bank robbers. I liked movies where women were shown as empowering themselves—even if, as in this case, they went about it the wrong way. But given each woman's set of circumstances, what else could they do?

I knew I'd never rob a bank myself, but I cheered on Queen Latifah, Jada Pinkett, Vivica Fox and Kimberly Elise as if they were my sisters. I was at the scene in the movie where I cry at every time—I already had my tissues out and was wiping my eyes and blowing my nose—the part where Queen Latifah got shot up by what looked like all of L.A.P.D. Suddenly my cell phone vibrated. *Who could this be?* I wondered, as I reached for it.

At first I didn't recognize the voice; it was so loud and out of control. "What? Who?" I kept saying. I could hear the loud clamor of voices in the background. Sniffing, I reached over and put my movie on pause.

Finally, I realized it was Shirley. I couldn't make out her words, between the screams and hollers, something I was not used to, since she always seemed in control. I had to ask her to repeat herself twice. "What did you say?" I still couldn't understand her.

About the third time, I finally made out what she was saying.

"Someone's shot Trayvon."

My heart dropped, and then the hammering started. "What? I'll be right there."

In a blind flurry of arms and legs locomoting through my small place, I frenetically flipped close the cell phone, grabbed my purse and car keys and barreled to the front house.

"Who called you?" I asked, as Shirley grabbed her London Fog trench coat.

"Southwest P.D." Her eyes were shooting wildly all over the place. "I thought his game was in Inglewood."

"I did too."

"What happened?"

"I don't know." I never saw Shirley look so helpless.

As we were leaving, I heard the baby, Brooklyn, crying, "My brother got shot," but Malibu, as always the mother figure, hushed her.

"He's going to be okay, Brooklyn."

They were all looking upset, and wanted to go to the hospital with us. We decided it would be too much to handle. We decided to leave the children at home. We didn't know what Trayvon's status was. I tried to remain calm in front of them.

I gunned my new, used Toyota Corolla and sped in a mad dash to Centinela Hospital in Inglewood, since Martin Luther King, the gun shot trauma hospital that used to be in Watts, had been shut down. Everything felt like a nightmare that I just couldn't wake up from. I was praying this couldn't be true, and if it were, that it wasn't too late. I ran through red lights, but thankfully the police never pulled me over.

My heart was beating so fast I was afraid I'd have a heart attack. My sweaty palms clenched the steering wheel so tightly, they almost felt numb when I finally swerved into the hospital parking lot, screeching to a halt.

As we arrived at the hospital, the guards sent us around to the back to get into the Emergency Room. Chica and her fiancé, Riley Whitmore, who I met for the first time, were already there in the corridor in the crowded Emergency Room.

Chica was laying in the floor kicking, and screaming, over and over, "Oh, God, no! Not my baby!" Meantime, Riley was trying to soothe her.

I figured then that it was worse than we thought.

"She won't get up," said Riley, Chica's fiancé, when he looked up, helplessly holding his hands in the air. He appeared distraught, but he recognized Shirley. "Someone's got to identify him." A nod of his head let me know the worse had happened.

That was when I knew Trayvon had expired. Finally Shirley and I decided to go in and identify the body. First, we talked to the doctor, a Dr. Bradley, who spoke in hushed tones. "We did all we could do. He was dead on arrival. You have my condolences. He was shot in the chest and he bled out."

"What was the time of death?" I asked.

"9:30 P.M."

We were finally escorted to a room off the emergency room where Trayvon was laying. The nurses had cleaned him up. He had a sheet pulled up to his neck. He looked so young, so vulnerable, almost like a little boy, with some height. His eyes were closed like he was sleeping and his body still felt warm to the touch.

I thought about when Trayvon came to me, saying he was afraid to go to school. Was this shooting related to the hit the Mexican gangs had supposedly put out on civilians?

A nurse came in, murmuring condolences, and handed us his clothes in a plastic bag. I noticed my Starter jacket. Dried blood was beginning to crust on the black background of the collar. I almost threw up.

It finally hit me. Trayvon was gone. That's when I broke down.

13

The day of Trayvon's funeral was the worst day of all of our lives. Although the sun fell in parallelograms with mote-swirling dust through the stained-glass church window, it was a dark day for us on the inside.

Burying Trayvon was not exactly how I had envisioned his life. I had always thought I would go to his high school, then college graduation. I'd always thought I'd see him go places in life. Not wind up in a bronze-colored casket before his life even got started. It took all my strength not to take a drink this past week before the funeral and the wake. So far, I'd been sober since I went into rehab—one day at a time. That cliché worked, too. *One day at a time*, I repeated to myself. Sometimes it was one minute at a time.

The smells of chrysanthemums filled my nostrils and added to my depression. The smell always reminded me of my father's funeral. I gazed up at the Black Jesus on the wall, and wondered, *When do we ever catch a break as a foster kid?* I knew Shirley taught me that life wasn't fair, but dayumm!

Most of Shirley's church members were present. A number of Trayvon's high school classmates filled the pews. His coach, Mr. Barry, the principal, Mr. Jackson, and a number of teachers filled the church. People were crying throughout the church. Young people held hands in a queue down each pew.

All week, shrines had been built around the street light near our house and down at the shopping center at Martin Luther King Boulevard and Crenshaw where he was killed. This was just across the street from Magic Johnson's Movie Theater where I used to take Trayvon and his sisters for the Saturday matinees.

Candlelight vigils were held on the streets almost every night the preceding days before the funeral. Neighbors had been swarming in and out the house with warmed dishes of fried chicken, El Pollo Loco grilled chicken, tortillas, collard greens, macaroni and cheese, trays of enchiladas, red beans and rice, and someone even baked a golden brown turkey. But none of the family had an appetite.

The *L.A. Times*, and all the black papers, *The Sentinel*, the *Wave* and the *L.A. Watts Times* were filled with headlines: "COMMUNITY GALVANIZES OVER SHOOTING OF HIGH SCHOOL NBA PROSPECT." "CITY IS IN SHOCK OVER MURDER OF NBA HOPEFUL."

Sadness gripped the Baldwin Hills Baptist Church where there was standing room only. The black mortuary has done a good job and Trayvon was buried wearing his basketball shirt and his team number. He was the star point guard on his team. His casket was surrounded by chrysanthemums and roses, making the smells of life and death rival each other.

Chica was so distraught, the church nurses had to carry her out within the first fifteen minutes. Riley, who had remained at her side throughout the whole ordeal, had to go outside and try to help calm her down. Malibu, Charisma, Brooklyn, and Soledad, all dressed in white dresses, were inconsolable. Trayvon's friend, Delonte, and a teenage girl, I assumed may have been

Trayvon's girlfriend, sat on the front row with the family. They both couldn't stop crying either.

A heavy-set singer named Cynthia sang such a beautiful rendition of CeCe Winan's "Don't Cry." She sounded like an angel.

I fought back my tears so I could be strong for the family. *I'll cry later,* I told myself. I understood the tears of those around me though. For how could you not help but cry? A good kid, college bound, wiped out. Why? No gang affiliations from what everyone said. When would this senseless violence end?

Everyone lost it all over again, when Chica's twelve-year old daughter, Malibu, sang, "Precious Lord." I didn't realize that child had such pipes—I mean she could really blow.

The funeral rushed by in a blur for me, but I was really touched when a local artist named Dr. Maxine Thompson delivered her poem.

"Son of God Called Home Too Soon"
You were not just some faceless young black boy,
   Barely turned fifteen,
   whose death was flashed on the news,
   No, you were our beloved son, our child, our oldest.
   Not only that, you were a cousin, a nephew and a friend to many.
   You also had many relatives, who loved you, too,
   But most of all, you were a son of God called home too soon.

   You were a seedling in the prime of life,
   Your entire life a leaf unfurling, pregnant with possibility,
   The things you could have done,

The places you could've gone,
More lives you could have touched,
But, no, it was not to be.

How many more of our young men must we
lose
   To acts of senseless violence and rage?
   When will we learn to love and not hate,
   To cherish and not exterminate?
   Let's wake up before it's too late
   And we lose our entire future Black race.

But, only God, in His wisdom, knows
When and why He calls us home too soon,
   Perhaps He says, "You were only on loan to
them, my son,
   You all are just renting your time in this earth-
ly space,
   As for you, Trayvon, I have prepared a better
place."

   That's why we must take our short allotted time
on earth
   To love deeply,
   Live fully,
   Give plentifully.

   In your fifteen years,
   You did this. You provided us with many mo-
ments of joy,
   Happiness and smiles.
   Trayvon, from your first breath to your last,
   From your first steps to your final ones, we
loved you.
   Your smile, your laugh, your love, we will al-
ways remember and cherish.

You will never be forgotten,
Love, Your mother and father, Maritza Olegari
and the late Ted (Dog Bite) Jackson

When the program called for remarks about the deceased, one by one, different classmates got up and gave their remarks about how they remembered Trayvon.

I glanced to the back of the church. I noticed a few known gangbangers, some of whom I recognized from when I was on the force. They had come in and sat in the back, but they seemed respectful, because from what I heard at the wake, they wanted to know who did this as well. The way they took off their scarves and caps, you could see they came in peace. I recognized known gang members from the Baldwin Village Bloods, the Long Beach Boulevard Crips, the Rolling Sixties, the Bounty Hunters and Pirus Bloods.

I looked back and recognized an O.G. Crip named F-Loc from Jordan Downs' Grape Street Crips. I got up and walked down the aisle. I beckoned to him through lifting my head. I vaguely remembered F-Loc from my childhood, but I mainly knew him from when I lived with Chica in Jordan Downs. He nodded his head in recognition. He let me know right away he remembered Mayhem, who was still incarcerated but had been transferred to Chino, from what he informed me.

F-Loc spoke in a low voice, his hand over his mouth, failing to hide his gold grill. "Yeah, I remember you, too. Mayhem's little sister." He eyed my curves and his gaze lingered at my hips, but I cut my eyes, letting him know this was no time for B.S. But, all the while, he was giving me respect. There was a level of reverence through association which brought to mind how Mayhem's rep and my mother's rep made me like some Ghetto Mafia princess when I was growing up.

"Did you know Trayvon?" I spoke under my breath, but I got straight to the point. "Did he have any gang affiliations?"

"Nah, Trayvon was a good kid. See, I live in the jungle now. We used to look out for him when he'd be out practicing ball or walking through the hood. We wanted to see him get in the NBA. We want to know who did this shit, too." There was a menacing glint in his eye and I hated to think of the street justice that might get served.

We exchanged cell phone numbers, then I tiptoed back up to the front of the church for the rest of the funeral.

Finally Pastor Patterson, sweat dripping from his forehead, took control of the pulpit, therefore the congregation, and a hush fell over the entire church. He really preached, to everyone who was in the church.

"When we look at this young man's remains before us," he paused for dramatic effect, "we know this is out of the natural order. All over our community, mothers are losing their sons to this senseless violence. Too much blood is running in the street and no one is crying out about it. If this were in the suburbs, there would be an uproar on the part of society, but our victims are black and brown."

Pastor Patterson paused again in a timely fashion for the traditional call and response.

"Preach, Rev. It's the truth anyhow."

"That's the word."

"Speak on it."

Pastor Patterson continued and his voice crescendoed. "We are the victims of the scourge of drugs, gangs and violence. This evil three is a pestilence sucking the life blood of the future from this city.

"Brown and black have to stop warring against one another. It's as if the violence has been outsourced to let the minorities kill one another.

"Teenagers are afraid to go to school. We now have a Safe Passage Program to help children get back and forth to school. Now, I don't know about you, but I think there is something wrong with this picture."

"Tell it like it is, Pastor," someone intoned.

Pastor took his fist and pounded on the pulpit. "We've got to take back control of our community and stop letting the gangs run it. The real men and women have to stand up. We've got to stop our kids from being afraid to wear different colors, blue or red. Now they are even threatening to kill anyone wearing white T-shirts. What kind of mess is this? Do y'all hear me?"

"We hear you, Pastor."

Pastor Patterson took his handkerchief and swiped his now sweating face. He continued his sermon, "Another one of our young slain." He shook his head vigorously, then wiped his big white handkerchief over his sopping wet forehead. "We must not rise in anger. We can't seek revenge. We've got to leave this in the Lord's hand. 'Vengeance is mine,' saith the Lord. We've got to rise up in hope for the future.

"For today I say to you, we are declaring war on these people who will not allow our young people to live to see eighteen. Are we afraid of these hoodlums? No, but we don't want you to go out and kill in retaliation. We want you to stop the killing and have peace."

Pastor Patterson ended on this note.

"We've talked about the dead, but I'm going to talk to the living. Now, I want to know this. What are you going to do? What will be your legacy? In Trayvon's short years, he touched a lot of people. He gave his life to Christ at an early age. Do you want to come to Christ today? What will be your legacy?"

A dozen people marched up and joined the church at this point.

After the funeral, as I was shambling out the church, I noticed Detective Gonzalez. Romero was standing inconspicuously in the back with a group of Latino students from the high school, so he did not stand out, other than he was older looking than the others. He was wearing mirrored shades, but I recognized him. He must have seen me studying him, because he nodded his head at me as I marched by.

When I passed his pew, he stepped in line and escorted me to the family funeral car. Outside, the sun was blinding white and I reached in my Coach bag and slid on my sunglasses. My head was pounding like a hammer on an anvil. It felt worse than some of my hangovers following a night of being "ten sheets to the wind."

"I see you're sitting with the family." He raised his eyebrow, and asked, "A relative of yours?"

"My nephew."

He let out a low whistle. "You have my condolences. Sorry for your loss."

I tipped my head in acknowledgment. "What are you doing here? Funny how we keep running into each other."

"This is part of a homicide investigation."

"I thought you were in Pacific Division."

"I am. But I'm also doing undercover, which might tie into this case. I'll check with the detective in charge over at Southwest."

"Any leads?"

"Not yet."

"Well, a few of his friends say two Latinos walked up and just smoked him."

"I'm so sorry. It's always the good kids. . . . I'd like to take you for coffee to talk about the case, whenever you're ready." He handed me a card, which had his cell phone number scribbled on the back. He held the door for me, and I climbed in with the rest of the family.

After the funeral, I rode in the family car limousine with Shirley, Chill, Chica, and the girls, on the half-hour trail to Inglewood Cemetery. A motorcade led the funeral procession and the line went on for several city blocks. All the car lights were on, and people moved over to the curb as we rode by, running through red lights, but moving at a slow, steady speed.

I sat on one side of Chica, holding her right hand. Chica kept leaning on Shirley, crying in gut wrenching sobs. They sounded so haunting, so animal-like. Her cries reminded me of a howling wolf. Primitive, lonely, ancient as time. A cry that must have gone back to the Middle Passage. A mother's grief.

All the while, Shirley patted her other hand, trying to control her own tears. Shirley had held up in her usual stoic manner, and, like me, had not broken down since the first night. She'd always been our pillar of strength.

"Mama, it hurts so bad." Chica gulped, trying to catch her breath between her cries. " I've never been there for Trayvon and now that I—I—I was getting myself together, this happens. Why him? Why not me? How can I go on?"

Shirley was quiet for a while. When she spoke up, she simply said, "With God's help."

14

Since we buried Trayvon, Chica was a mess. I was afraid she was going to relapse or have a nervous breakdown. She was losing it. When I visited Chica at her and Riley's apartment in North Hollywood, she couldn't stop crying. I was so afraid she was going to start using again, I got nervous, but Riley said she hadn't.

The truth be known, I'd been tempted to take a drink myself, but so far, I hadn't. I knew it would only make matters worse. And that was, and remained, Shirley's one rule for me renting her spot. I had to stay clean and sober.

Fortunately, the FOR SALE sign had gone down at the big house. Unfortunately, though, when I went to visit the big house, Shirley was a zombie, which was worse than Chica, who was at least getting her pain out. I hadn't seen my foster mother cry since the night at the hospital.

The whole house screamed of Trayvon's absence. No one had touched his bedroom, which he'd shared with no one since he was the only boy. The same Michael Jordan, Shaq and Kobe posters, and the same eleven by eighteen inch pictures of his team winning the championship last year still decorated his walls. His many trophies graced the top of his dresser. I got a chill as I walked by his room and peeked in. So much young energy gone. The house just felt weird.

Shirley had been sequestered in her room since the funeral. Even Chill had gotten worried about her and he came shuffling out of his room, where he had spent the past few years, locked up, except for when he wanted his meal on a TV tray. His speech was halting, as he met me in the hallway. "Something's wrong with Shirley. She hasn't fed me." I didn't pay his broken speech any attention. I was used to it. Still, it saddened me to remember how Daddy Chill used to have a sharp mind before he retired from the Post Office. I guess he was just getting old.

I wandered into the kitchen where the girls were wandering around the house and bumping into each other like blind guppies. In the past week, I'd cooked simple meals like hamburgers for them and tried to help with their homework, but I was not exactly mother material. This particular evening, Malibu, at age 12, was cooking sloppy joes so I let out a sigh of relief.

"Malibu, can you give Daddy Chill a sloppy joe, too?"

She nodded, looking too ancient for her years. I hated when people dumped so much on the oldest girl in a family. It didn't matter how large the family was either. It reminded me of my first nine years with Venita. When she gave birth to Diggity, it was as if I had given birth to a baby. She handed him over to me, and I had to get up with him at night, although I was only eight. I carried that boy on my hip so much, it still jutted out on one side to this day.

Unfortunately, everyone was falling apart at the same time. Quiet as it was kept, I was just holding on by a gossamer thread myself, but I wanted to try to do something to help out.

"G-Ma hasn't been eating," Malibu said, face scrunched up like she was the mother of five, instead of a carefree twelve-year-old girl.

I didn't say anything as I opened a can of chicken soup, heated it and put it on a tray. I turned to Malibu. "Don't worry. I'll feed Shirley. Feed the kids and Daddy Chill."

I climbed the stairs and timidly knocked on Shirley's bedroom door. "Moochie, can I talk to you?"

When no one answered, I pushed the door open. The room was so dark, I stumbled over her house shoe laying strewn in the walkway.

Shirley was lying on her bed, on top of her brocade spread, which she raised us saying was a 'no-no'. The shutters were closed, the drapes pulled. Her Afro twists, which were peppered with gray, hadn't been tied up and they looked as tangled as a grapevine. Her gown was hanging off her once size-twelve frame. She looked like she'd lost about fifteen or twenty pounds.

It was a good thing she took an early retirement from the school board when Chica dropped the last baby, or she would be fired from her job.

As I stepped inside her room, I shuttered my eyes with both hands to adjust to the darkness, then I peered around. Everything looked dim. Her generally green plants that she kept in her bedroom were dying. I turned on the Tiffany lamp light in the corner.

"Cut it off," Shirley snapped. With a flick of my wrist, I turned the lights back out.

"Well, excuse me," I apologized.

I was grieving too, but I knew one thing that had become my mantra. *I cannot take a drink, I cannot take a drink, I cannot take a drink.*

The truth was, I was feeling more pain than when Okamoto died. I stayed so wasted for about the first nine months, I was numb to my pain. Whenever I thought about Okamoto I'd get drunk. This time, when death came a knocking through young Trayvon, I was blown completely out the water. Here I was, working on my recovery, and then this. I knew that recovery was supposed to be a good thing, but, coupled with this pervading feeling of doom brought on by our grief, I felt a knife twisting in my gut at all times.

How could life be so cruel, so unjust? I knew Shirley always taught us life wasn't fair, but this was a dirty blow to all of us who knew Trayvon. Why him and not us? What kind of God would allow this type of thing to happen? I had to fight hard not just to slip into this darkness which was like a big maul as wide and gaping as the grave they buried Trayvon's youthful body in.

I put the tray on Shirley's nightstand, then flung open the drapes and the windows to let in some air and sunlight. "Moochie," I called her in a soft voice. "Are you awake?"

Shirley had her lower arm thrown over her eyes to keep the sun from blinding her. She was quiet for the longest time. Just when I was about to give up and call her name again, I heard Shirley's voice. It sounded gravelly, as if she were lying in a grave. For the first time, I was afraid I was going to lose her too. I had to do something. What would all of us do without Shirley?

"I can't believe my grandson is gone. He had so much to live for."

I tried to say words of comfort, but I knew they were useless as I spoke them. "Com'on now. Trayvon wouldn't want you to give up. You've got the other kids looking at you."

"I keep seeing him saying good-bye to us. It's as if he knew something—the way he looked back at us."

A chill rippled through me. I shivered. Goose bumps rose on my arms. I nodded, and didn't say anything. I'd thought about his last look often too, but I didn't want to get Shirley any more worked up than she was. I didn't know which was worse. Maybe Shirley would have been better off to cry every day since she only cried that one time at the hospital. The way things looked, it was just like she'd shut down. I was afraid we'd lose her if she didn't snap out of it.

"I can't sleep. I can't eat. I'm like that spider plant just hanging from the ceiling. I'm just here, but I wish I were dead. I've never hurt this badly."

"Moochie, you've got to eat," I urged.

"I'm not hungry."

"Remember when Chica and I both had the chicken pox and you had to make us eat? Come on now."

I tried to spoon feed Shirley some of the soup, and she only sipped a tad bit down. She shook her head and pushed the bowl away from her. I decided to take control of the situation. "Shirley, get up."

"I can't get up." Her voice sounded weak, hopeless, not like the Shirley I'd always known. This was not the woman who picked me up out the dumps after my father's death and my mother's imprisonment. Not the woman, who sat through my detox until I got my head on straight.

Now the roles had reversed. "Look, Moochie, pull yourself together."

Shirley just stared ahead at the ceiling. "You can't tell me how to feel."

"Well, you're acting worse than Chica."

"Look, just because I didn't birth Trayvon, I'm the one who sat up all night when he came home from the hospital at four and a half pounds, all cracked out from his mama. I'm the one who taught him to read at three, when they said he would be damaged because of the crack. Trayvon is—was my son. Just because you birth a child doesn't make you the mother."

"I'm sorry. I didn't mean it that way."

Suddenly Chill interrupted us, breaking into the room, and brought the old-fashioned house phone to me. "This is for Shirley."

"Go way." Shirley waved her hand lethargically.

I took the phone and heard a frantic voice spilling out. "Shirley, it's an emergency. It's Haviland."

"Oh, hi. This is Z."

"What are you doing there?"

"Long story."

"Were you kin to Trayvon?" Haviland asked.

"Yes. I was his auntie."

"Well, I'm sorry to hear about him."

"Thank you."

"I know it's late, but I need a place to stay. Long story, too, but can I rent a room there for about a month?"

I turned to Shirley. She took the phone out my hand. "I don't want no monkey business now, Haviland. You can move here until you get on your feet." I was surprised Shirley agreed.

As she clicked the phone shut, I said, "I never told Haviland that I lived here. Since we got out the program I always met her out at places."

"Why not?"

"I just don't trust her."

"Well, we have to give people a chance, Z." She looked at me pointedly, as if to remind me how she gave me a second chance.

"All right. You're right." I changed the subject to something I'd been meaning to ask Shirley. "I know you said you knew her mother, but how did you get to know Haviland?"

"Her mother used to volunteer at McLaren Hall, when I would volunteer. Sometimes she brought Haviland with her." Shirley sat up erectly, swinging her legs over the side of the bed.

She continued. "Her mother told me what a problem Haviland had been since she was a teen. On drugs. In and out of rehab for the past ten years. It's a shame— with all that education." Shirley shook her head.

I knew what a headache Haviland could be, and I really felt Shirley was too weak to take her on. So it was decided. "As much as I hate to do it, Haviland can stay with me. I'll let her sleep on the cot."

Shirley threw her hands in the air. "I didn't sign up for this. When did my house become a boarding house?" Even so, I could hear some of the old fight coming back in her voice.

"When you opened your doors."

Shirley finally stood up, took a long stretch, and let out a deep "whew." She pulled her shoulders back and stretched, feline-like.

"I'm going to take a shower. Whew! I smell."

I don't know where it came from, but I spoke out and said something I hadn't planned to say. "Moochie, I'm going to find out who killed Trayvon, if it's the last thing I do."

Shirley turned to me and nodded. Her head was held high, like a new resolve had come over her. I watched her transform before my eyes as she marched into her private bathroom off her bedroom.

I hoped I could deliver on my promise. And then it hit me. I hoped it was not the last thing I lived to do.

15

I planned to go to the high school as soon as possible after the funeral and do some investigating, but everything seemed frozen into a mold of grief. I couldn't seem to move forward and I couldn't seem to move backwards. After making the promise to Shirley, I forced myself to drive to Dorsey High School to poke around and see what I could find, but changed my mind after I arrived. I wound up sitting in my car and never getting out. I was just too raw inside to ask any questions yet.

I'd done homicide investigations before, but the decedents were strangers. This was different. Trayvon was family.

Instead, I drove to a nearby bar and sat outside. I wanted a drink so badly, my mouth sluiced a stream of saliva. I could already feel the first cool guzzle of a beer going down my throat. I knew this was crazy, but this taking life straight with no chaser was more than I could stand.

I felt like I had an alter-ego sitting on my shoulder, egging me on. "You deserve a drink. You've been through hell. You've dried out and your system could probably handle one or two drinks. Yeah. Just get a couple of beers to knock the chill off. You won't get drunk this time."

This was really what I wanted to hear.

But then there was my better self whispering in my other ear. "Z, you know you can never drink again. You will die if you drink. Period. Dot. Dash. Go sit your ass down somewhere."

I didn't know what to do. I was torn between wanting to take a drink and wanting to stay sober. I never was a religious person, even when Shirley took us to church nearly every Sunday, but this was one time, I found myself praying.

"Higher Power, God, Jehovah, Allah, please help me not go in there and take a drink. If I do, it will destroy everything I've accomplished in the past few months in one day. Amen."

I didn't know what happened, but lo and behold, a police car pulled up behind to give me a parking ticket. "Miss, don't you see the 'No Parking' sign? Today is street cleaning day."

I let out a sigh of relief. I had never been happier in my life to get a parking ticket. When I was a cop, I'd flash my badge and get out of the ticket. But this time, I took the ticket gratefully because, as quickly as the urge had come on, the urge for a drink had passed.

"Thank you, Lord," I said, looking up. Is this what the twelve-step program meant by surrendering? I surely couldn't handle this desire to drink on my own. I guess it would take a higher power. I guess the Lord intervened in my behalf. This let me know that I couldn't get too confident. I was not running this sobriety show on my own power.

I drove off instead of going into the bar.

I pulled over when I turned the corner, and called F-Loc on my cell phone, but he didn't answer. He didn't have a voice mail set up, and I can imagine why. All the dealers knew that cell phones could be used as evidence against you. They'd even learned how to scramble-up codes on beepers now to fool the police.

A few days later, I decided to go to the barber shop, Scissors and Shaves, to get the low-down. I'm telling you, the black barber shop kept an ear to the streets better than any confidential informant could. If anything was happening, the men sitting around would know.

Mac, my barber, who kept my short crop in a style similar to Halle Berry's hair cut she wore when she won the Academy Award, had me wait about a half hour before he slid me into the chair.

I was glad, because I was looking for information. I sat and soaked in the conversation like a sponge. This was the nice thing about them never knowing that I was a police officer even when I was on the force. I never wore my uniform home, and I didn't even let my neighbors know.

I waited for the signifying and the loud talk to begin. When a game came on the little seventeen-inch TV, it was on and popping then.

"Yeah, Kobe is the reason the Lakers is gon' go to the championship this year." A regular named T-Bone threw out his opinion as fact when the first quarter almost ended.

"Aw, you ain't no psychic," a younger man named Butch countered. "You don't know shit from shinola."

I tuned them out as they argued the merits of the Lakers and the Clippers, until I zeroed in on what I wanted to hear.

"Did y'all hear about the shooting last weekend? Some Crips blasted some Mexicans."

"Where, man?"

"Down in the jungle." Baldwin Village, better known as the Jungle, was known for its crime activity. The area was made famous in the movie *Training Day*— the apartments where Denzel went to see his "lovely dime"—his outside "affair" girlfriend and baby mama.

"What were they doing in the jungle?"

"You know how they killed that fourteen-year-old girl in Harbor City back in January?"

"And remember that boy whose mama had to be flown in from Iraq to bury her own son?"

"That was Jamiel Shaw. Wasn't he that football star at Crenshaw High? Ain't nobody talking about it, but there's been a lot of brown on black killings and vice-versa."

"And it's all over those drugs. Word is that the Mexican cartels runs more shit from the prison than on the streets. Ain't that a motha? They can reach out and touch your ass from the pen."

Everyone fell silent, as if they knew they were talking too much.

"Quiet as it's kept, there's been a whole lot of murders every weekend here lately." Lo-Jack, another regular who was about in his forties, said in a hushed tone.

I just sat and listened, filing away the information. Were these random killings? Or had there been a rise in retaliation murders since Trayvon's death? Were they all related? What was going on?

After I left the barber shop, I shot over to Dorsey High School, from where I graduated in '92. This time, in spite of my grief-stricken haze, I forced myself to go inside.

Everything seemed smaller since I attended here. The corridors seemed narrower, the stairwell seemed shorter, the smells seemed less chalky than my memory. The school now had computer labs. However, the girls were larger. Most of them appeared to be over a size sixteen, and had huge pendulous breasts and butts like grown women. Dang, what's in the water? This processed food was leading to a generation of Amazons.

Anyhow, I strolled to the principal's office, and show him my private investigator's license and my driver's license. He remembered me from the funeral.

"Did Trayvon have any gang affiliations?" I asked. I had to take everything into consideration. You never knew what kids did when they weren't in your face.

"No. No gang affiliations. No tattoos. No juvy record. An eyewitness says there were two Latino males who came up and shot him in the chest, execution style." Mr. Jackson shook his head, ruefully, lacing and unlacing his fingers "How's the family holding up?" he asked.

"We're holding on." I eyed him in a way to let him know that I was family.

"Tell them they are in my prayers. We all miss Trayvon. He had so much potential." He heaved a deep sigh of remorse. "I just don't know what this world's coming to."

He gave me permission to interview some of Trayvon's friends. As I trudged down the hall, I thought of how death made us all uncomfortable—particularly an untimely death through murder of a young person. I finally located Delonte, Trayvon's friend, hanging around his locker, obviously skipping class.

"I thought you were supposed to be in Chemistry, Delonte?"

Delonte looked kind of sheepish. "I know. I'm going, Miss Z."

"Yeah, it takes a minute to get used to what is, but you've got to keep going. Okay?"

Delonte's lips were trembling, as he nodded in agreement. "I've got a question for you. What happened that night?"

"We had a scrimmage game that night. Anyhow, my mother's car broke down so we caught the Crenshaw bus home. I saw Tray get off at MLK and as soon as he got off the bus, two Mexicans just came up outta nowhere and shot him." He teared up, just thinking of it.

"What did you do?" A chill coursed through me. What if they'd shot Delonte too? The boy didn't realize how lucky he'd been.

"I pounded on the window and made the bus driver let me off. He pulled over too and a lot of people got off to try to help Trayvon. I used my cell phone to call the police." Delonte tried to cover his tears by putting his elbow up to his eyes.

"That was brave of you. They could have gone after you."

"No, they jumped in a dark car and pulled off."

"Do you remember what kind of car it was?"

"No, just that it was dark."

I patted Delonte on the shoulder, trying to soothe him. "You did all you could do."

After a while, I ask, "Is that all you remember? Did Trayvon have a girlfriend?"

"Yeah. They've been liking each other since junior high."

"What is her name?"

"Tai."

"Do you know what class she'd be in?"

Delonte shrugged. "She's a cheerleader, so she might be at practice."

"Go back to class, Delonte. Trayvon wouldn't want you to give up. Stay in school."

Next, I went back to the office and found the field where the cheerleaders were practicing. Tai was one of the few petite cheerleaders on the team. Many of the girls are what they call "thick" now a days.

"Tai, do you know if Trayvon had any enemies?"

She started crying, large tears glazing her eyes and rolling down her nut brown cheeks. "No. Everyone loved Tray. He was good people. We'd plan to go to college together like Tre and Brandi in the movie, 'Boys in the Hood.' We were gonna get married after we finished school."

"Okay, Tai. Don't cry. We're going to get to the bottom of this. We're going to get justice."

I really wasn't so sure of myself. I knew L.A.P.D. had files and files of cold cases where murders had never been solved.

The more time elapsed after the murder, the less chance of catching the murderer.

I felt like Delonte and Tai knew more than they were telling me, but I couldn't get it out of them.

Anyhow, I was going to give this investigation my all. I had to find out who killed my nephew, if at all possible.

I just had no idea where to start. What was I going to do?

16

"Why don't you guys all go to the bereavement meeting?" Joyce, who continued to be my sponsor, suggests when I tell her the aftermath of Trayvon's death. "Everyone has to grieve in his or her own way, but a bereavement service will help you have a sense of closure that a funeral doesn't always provide."

Since I was kind of at a stand still as to what to do about Trayvon because I was still depressed, I agreed with Joyce. I invited Chica, Shirley and the girls to a bereavement group, which I personally needed for myself for my grief over both Trayvon and Okamoto. I felt this would help with my nagging thirst for another drink too.

Meantime, Chica's and Riley's wedding was postponed because she was too distraught and grief-stricken. Truthfully, I thought that was for the best. It was just too soon to be celebrating a new life together.

Since Haviland moved in my apartment and she was only supposed to be with me a month, I asked her to go to the bereavement service with us. I didn't trust her to be going through my things when I was not there. Basically, she was only in my apartment when I was there at night, because she spent her days going on auditions for parts on TV or any movies she hoped she could land. This evening she was tired because she'd spent her entire day trying to get a role in a Lifetime made for TV movie about a character she said had the big *C*—cancer.

According to Haviland, she'd barely gotten past page one when the casting director called "Next!" In her usual dramatic fashion, Haviland rolled her eyes toward the ceiling. She said she wanted to tell the casting director, "My dear, I don't give a damn," when she didn't get the part, but instead, she held her head up with dignity and marched out.

"Come on and ride with me. This will be good for you," I said. She looked happy to be included.

Haviland had her own struggles. She was trying to stay clean and get back into 'the business' as she called show business, which was almost an oxymoron, so I figured it wouldn't hurt for her to go to the meeting with us. She could grieve her old life as an A-list actress, or even the fact her birth mother died from AIDS a month after their reunion. She and her adoptive mother were still estranged, so she needed a family support system too. I guess life was just a series of losses.

Riley accompanied Chica, and they met us at the service. The bereavement meeting took place in Torrance at an office building near Vermont. They had all types of people, from all races and creeds, who were there grieving. You could almost feel the pain in the room, the grief was so palpable.

The room was decorated with white candles, crepe paper, and live calla lilies. A guitar player was present and he sang in a folksy sounding way and reminded me of the old Peter, Paul, and Mary group. My mind hushed as I took in the candlelight service. The moderator, Miss Lyons, stood up and spoke at the podium.

"Grief knows no season. It is a natural reaction to losing a loved one. You're all here because you want to get help, and know that what you are going through is normal—under the circumstances."

I gazed around the room. All types of people were there grieving. Young, old, and in between. One by one, people got up and gave their testimonies. Afterwards, they lit a candle in the person's memory.

An older Caucasian man, who said he'd been married sixty-seven years, broke down and bawled like a baby during his testimony over his recently departed spouse. I guess that was a long time to have been married—which I wouldn't know since I hadn't made it past the first year.

A stoic Jamaican woman, whose son died from AIDS at thirty-five, shared her story—how they prepared for his death for fifteen years, and how she, as a nurse, was able to provide hospice for her dying son.

A widowed Latino mother, along with her two sons, age ten, and eleven, stood up. She'd lost her husband and their father to pancreatic cancer earlier in the year. She related how she and her two sons visited his grave and took the son's first A report cards since their father's death.

One by one, everyone, except Chica and me, got up and talked about Trayvon.

Shirley spoke first. "To lose a child before yourself is not only out the natural order of life, it is one of the deepest sorrows you can ever know.

"Although I didn't carry Trayvon under my heart, I've carried him in my heart since he was born. Trayvon, you'll always live in our hearts. Baby, we love you."

Brooklyn lit her candle, and spoke in a lisp. "I miss you, Trayvon, but I'll always love you. I'm keeping your basketball until I get to Heaven."

Haviland got up and gave her speech. "Jill, I never knew you other than when you carried me under your heart. I guess I never forgot you. I didn't get to know you before you died. I'll miss you." She lit her candle.

On the program we followed, poems were read and old songs accompanied by a guitar.

But what moved me the most was a short piece of prose in the program called, *The Grief Within:*

The grief within a person has its own heartbeat, its own life, its own song. Part of a person wants to fight the manifestations of grief. Yes, as a person surrenders to the song, they learn to listen deep within themselves. Let the life of this journey be just what it is—confusing, complicated, and at times overwhelming. A person must keep opening and changing through it all until they become the unique person who has transcended the pain and discovered self-compassion, a vulnerable yet grounded self who chooses to live again. Our sorrow reminds us that life is not to avoid pain and that to love is to accept the risk of hurting.

We were never promised joy without pain, sun without rain or roses without thorns. May we gain wisdom through our suffering, learn to have patience and take the time to work through our feelings. May we gain understanding and be in touch with the inner resources hidden within us. May we be guided through the future by gently transforming our grief into compassion, our hurts into new hope for ourselves and others. –Author Unknown

Nancy Vann's quote was equally inspiring:

"If you truly understand that we are only here for a short time, we will tend to waste less time on nonsense in order to pursue the quality of life you were put here to have."

Besides Chica, I was the only one who didn't get up and testify. "I'm too overcome," I said, throwing my hand up to pass.

Chica couldn't talk; she was so broken up. I couldn't talk because I didn't want to go back to that space where I first was when Trayvon was murdered.

I guess from habit, I kept my feelings bottled inside. I was still not telling the full truth. How did you go on when you felt responsible for someone's death? Even worse, now I was responsible for two deaths: my father's and Okamoto's. How do you live with the guilt?

Slowly, I could feel some of the guilt easing. Maybe I could not change what happened, but I could change how I felt about my father's and Okamoto's deaths. I was going to try to release my guilt about their deaths. In the case of Trayvon, I was going to have to put my grief aside so I could make progress with his murder investigation. And most of all, I'd have to make peace with my past.

Just coming here was helpful for me. After the ceremony, I felt a weight lifted off my shoulders. I noticed, as we left the center, we were all feeling better. Everyone, except me, had wept. They'd all talked about Trayvon, and had spoken about happier times. We all finally realized he would live on in our memory, and although the hurting hadn't stopped, I think the healing had begun.

After the meeting, Chica turned to me. "Shirley told me that you're trying to find Trayvon's murderer."

I nodded.

"Any new information?"

"Not yet. But I'm beginning to get some leads." I put my arms around Chica. "Don't worry. We'll find that bastard."

We walked out to the parking lot in much better spirits. Nightfall had arrived while we were in the building, but the parking lot was well lit. Just as I walked up to my car, I noticed shards of glass splattered on the ground.

"Oh, my God!" My front windows were smashed out. "What now?"

Once I climbed inside my car, I found a note using pasted on letters from a magazine on my dashboard. "Next time, we won't miss. You're next, bitch."

17

"Who do you think would do something like this, Z?" Haviland asked, after we called the Torrance P.D., who came out, and took a police report. I hid the death threat note in my purse, and just reported the vandalism.

"I don't know." But inside, I was perturbed. "What did they mean by next time we won't miss?" Was this a random act of violence? Or was there actually someone after me? And did they mean next after Trayvon? Who out in Torrance would know about Trayvon's murder? Was someone following me? Who could have sent me the death threat?

That night after we returned home, I went to bed, tossing and turning. I was glad I had car insurance to take care of the damage, but that's not what was bothering me.

Once again, I had my recurring nightmare about my father, only this time my father was alive. "The answer is inside you, little girl," he said to me. It was as if I was still a little girl. I was so happy and I reached out. "Daddy, I'm so glad you're back."

Just as I reached out my hand to him, I woke up from my dream, disappointed. I tried to figure out the meaning of my dream, but I couldn't. I went back to sleep.

I woke up with a new resolve in my spirit. I was going to have to start somewhere. I combed the newspapers to see if I could find a pattern of retaliation killings which began happening since Trayvon's murder, but I couldn't tell. This past weekend, there had been several types of homicides or drive-bys throughout the county, which was, sad to say, almost a norm for L.A. The media reported them, if they reported them at all, as random homicides, albeit some were gang-related. I thought about contacting the police. Nah, that would be too embarrassing. I was still ashamed about getting fired. I never wanted to see anyone from the police again—unless it was Romero. There was something about him that kept staying on my mind.

I put in a call to Romero's office line, but I got his answering machine. I left a message. "Romero, it's Z." I hesitated, as I didn't want to leave too much information on the business line's phone. "Call me. It's important."

I decided to call F-Loc again. "What it do?" he answered this time.

"F-Loc, Z here."

"Wait a minute, shorty. I understand you the law. I ain't no snitch nigga now."

"Confidential Informant," I corrected him "Besides, I haven't been with the force for over a year so this does not qualify you as a snitch. All this is off the record. I'm doing this as family. Trayvon was my nephew."

F-Loc hesitated for a moment, then he spoke up with feeling. "You know we all cared about young blood out here, and we wanted to see him make something of himself. We want some street justice too."

"Can we meet and talk?"

"Mickey D's on La Brea and Rodeo, and I don't mean the white Rodeo. Tomorrow." He clicked his phone shut.

F-Loc was referring to a little local humor where Black people called Martin Luther King Boulevard. West of

the Jungle, Ro—de—o and the white people called Rodeo Drive in Beverly Hills, "Ro-day-oh."

The next day, I met F Loc at a MacDonald's near the
corner of Rodeo and La Brea.

F-Loc had two goons with him who frisked me for
a wire, and holding my hands up high, I submitted to
their search with a nod of head, like "Cool."

"She cool, C-Note," one of the goons said, when he
finished scouring me.

F-Loc nodded at his flunkies. "Y'all can wait outside."

I sat down next to him in a booth across from him. I
always liked to sit with my eyes facing the front door—
a habit from being an officer. I was constantly looking
over my shoulder, but I got right to the point. "Have
you heard anything about Trayvon's murder on the
street?"

"Yeah, they say two Mexicans just came up and blasted that civilian when he got off the bus at Crenshaw and
MLK. This looks like a case of wrong place at the wrong
time. But there's something else."

"What?" I leaned forward. An icy thunderbolt zig-
zagged up my back. "What else have you heard?"

"Yeah, they say some Crips stole a large quantity of
drugs from a large cartel of the Mexican Mafia. Since
then, they've put out random hits on black civilians to
send out a message."

I froze. This was the second time I'd heard that. I
remembered how Trayvon had come to me, before he
died, saying he was afraid to go to school. Could the ru-
mor of the ordered hits be behind Trayvon's murder? I
needed to find out if I could find that connection.

"Huh?"

"It's not just the riots going on in the prison between black and brown. In different Mexican neighborhoods, they want to run blacks out. 'Ethnic cleansing.' Like that Cheryl Green case in Harbor City."

I murmured, "Mmmm."

"Something else, Z. Totally unrelated."

"Some strange shit went down the night of the Collin's shooting of that cop. You need to go see Pookie."

"Who's Pookie?"

"Larry Collins—the one who supposedly shot your partna."

I thought back to that crazy night—"Unca Pookie" as the little boy Shirrell had called the suspect, Lawrence Collins. I'd thought that was a done deal—a closed case. But was it?

"What do you mean supposedly?"

Something hit me in my gut. What was going on? "Do you know where he's at?"

"He still ain't gone to trial yet. He keeps getting continuances so he's probably still in County."

"You got anything else? You know, I notice there's been a lot of Latinos getting killed over the weekends. "

F-Loc scratched his imaginary beard, and peered over his sunglasses, which meant he was through talking for the day. He wouldn't say another word.

So, what if these recent Latino killings hadn't been random? Were these retaliation killings?

F-Loc cleared his throat. "Maybe you need to see your brother and find out what's going on out here. It's some funky shit going down. That's all I got to say."

"I haven't been in touch with Mayhem for years."

For years, I'd heard Mayhem was a Kingpin in the drug world as well as had his Crips affiliation. When I was a cop, occasionally, I'd checked his rap sheet. It was always filled with RICO charges and suspected murder allegations, but many of these charges wound up being dropped because the witnesses would suddenly mysteriously disappear.

"He's in Chino now, and I heard he might be getting out in a minute, I believe. It's something about some shit that goes all the way up to the top in high places and you need to see about it, y'understand? Mayhem might be able to tell you or send you to someone. I think it has to do with your partner's murder."

My heart flip flopped. I could feel my pulse speed up. I tried to remember that night, but so much had been lost and so many brain cells killed when I went on my binge, I just didn't know anything. What was there I needed to know? What was going on? My guts started flip flopping and I remembered Daddy Chill's words. "Trust your guts."

Something was going on, but what was it?

18

My cell phone rang and as if I'd called him onto my radar, it was Romero. "I got your call," he said. "What is it?"

"Can I meet you at Starbucks in Ladera Heights?" I asked since that was near Baldwin Hills.

"Sure. I'm off today." I heard Romero sneeze on the other end of the phone.

"Bless you."

"Thanks! It's going to take a minute to get there."

" Where do you live?"

"Silver Lake."

I don't know why I got so excited, but I took my time picking out my best pair of silk slacks, a vintage fitted black jacket, and a nice camisole with care. I wore fitted boots that came up to my knees and fold down. I ran my fingers through my hair, and I studied myself in the mirror.

I was still looking sad, but my skin looked better since I stopped drinking. In fact, my eyes were clearer than ever. No more bloodshot eyes. No more hangovers. I sure didn't miss those. I thought about a drink, but this time, I didn't have the same thirst for it. *One day at a time.*

Although Romero and I were not calling this a date—he realized I was still in mourning—it seemed like one in a crazy way. I had mixed feelings. I was wondering why I was so happy to see this guy, but on the other hand, now I could understand why some of the family members of murdered victims I met while I was a cop used to grieve so long. Even as a child, I grieved my father's death for many years. In fact, I still grieved for him.

I guess murder was worse than a natural death. You wanted someone to pay for taking your loved one's life away. Since Trayvon's murder, I felt like I was walking around in a fog, but I had to push forward. I was more determined than ever to find out who killed my nephew.

Around three that afternoon, Romero and I met at the Starbucks in Ladera Heights, which was considered another Black Beverly Hills section of L.A., but we were in the same parking lot as Magic Johnson's TGIF, Block Buster, a few markets, Ross's, and a drug store. The lot was filled with female and male bikers, a few B list actors, and writers. I assumed they were writers because they had their lap tops, and they were typing away as if the "Great American Novel," was just a key strike away. An eclectic mix of Los Angelinos I guess you'd call it.

Romero was already sitting on the patio when I arrived. He held out my seat, which I noted. Mmmm. A gentleman. He still possessed this cool exterior, like he'd been around the block. He was wearing his shades, and I sensed there was a lot beneath the surface. I noticed a few people staring at us, but interracial dating started here in California, (heck, we could go back to Sammy Davis, Jr. and May Britt), so they didn't even need to go there. Romero ordered Pumpkin Spice Frappucino and I ordered a Green Tea. I was trying not to get too hooked on coffee since I went on the wagon, because, truthfully, caffeine made me high.

Finally, I broached the subject. "Can I trust you, Romero?"

"What do you think?"

I thought back to how he gave me the ride home when he was a complete stranger and how he could have taken advantage of me. "I guess so."

I explained how I was trying to look for Trayvon's killer. I almost started to tell him what F-Loc told me about Pookie, but I held my tongue. Right now I was not sure who I could trust.

Who could I talk to? Where could I start? I had to find out who killed my nephew.

"You heard anything about Trayvon's murder?"

"No, but I'm checking it out. "

"Do you think this is a brown on black murder thing? Seems like that's happening more and more."

Romero glanced away from me, his jaws twitching. He seemed conflicted. I could understand how he felt torn, because I often felt torn as a cop when the perpetrators were black and I had to kick ass. He was Latino and he didn't seem to want to say it was his people who were the drive by shooters. Just like most of my community was peopled by law abiding citizens, most of the Latino community were hard-working citizens or immigrants. It was just the bad apples who gave everybody a bad name.

Romero kept his gaze on the table and didn't seem to want to look me in the eye. "You know this is a police matter and I'm not at liberty to discuss some of the facts. You should leave this alone and let the police handle it."

"Oh, cut the crap, Romero. I'm a licensed private investigator now." I flashed my credentials for him. "Besides that, this isn't some animal who was murdered. Trayvon is a human being. He's my people." I could hear my voice cracking with emotion. I spoke as if Trayvon were still alive. I didn't want to use the past tense with him yet . . . that made his death so permanent.

"I'm sorry, but I thought Chica was just your foster sister."

Pissed, I rolled my eyes at Romero. "Look, love doesn't have any stipulations on it or any rules. It just is. I love Chica. We grew up like sisters, so I loved her son. Now are you going to help me or not?"

Before I knew it, I was crying hysterically. I hadn't cried since the hospital so I didn't even know where this was coming from. I felt Romero put his arms around me. He rubbed me on the back, and then he kissed me. It was a tentative kiss, as if he was afraid to let loose, but I recognized this was more than a friendly kiss.

Not realizing how upset I was, I began to tongue Romero back like his tongue was manna in the desert and I was one of the Israelites. His tongue tasted so good, kind of minty, and kind of like the Frappucino. For a moment, I forgot my grief. Then, I remembered where we were.

I pulled away from Romero's embrace and saw some of the Starbucks staff and patrons staring at us.

"Com'on let's go," Romero took me by the elbow and led me to the parking lot. When we reached my car, he said, "We've got to see each other, Z. I know this is messed up. I've thought about you all these years, and sometimes I thought I'd imagined you. I know this isn't the time or place, but can we go to dinner sometime? That is—whenever you feel up to it."

"Not right now. Let me get through what I'm going through and we'll see."

After I drove off from the parking lot, I headed west down Centinela, planning to stop at the Fox Hills Mall just to lighten my mood. Without warning, a dark car with tinted windows almost ran into me from behind. I pulled up in time to keep the car from hitting me. At first I thought it was a near accident. But when I pulled off, the car pulled off behind me. Was this a carjacking? I sped up to get away from the car, and the car sped up. I changed lanes, the car changed lanes.

"What do you want from me?" I screamed out loud.

I made a sharp right turn as I reached Valley Ridge Street and hid between the many apartment complexes in Culver City. I sat ducked down in my seat on a side street for about twenty minutes. My heart was galloping, my pulse was racing, and I couldn't calm down. I waited. I watched the dark car circling around several times, then pass the street where I was hiding. The car wasn't close enough to get the license plate. I waited about another half hour.

Finally I drove back onto Valley Ridge. I kept staring into my rear view mirror, as I ducked and dodged, driving down Centinela. I headed west, away from Baldwin Hills. I passed Fox Hill Mall and kept going until I was sure no one was following me. I took deep breaths, trying to calm down my heart palpitations. My blouse was clinging to my back, I was so drenched in sweat. I wiped my hands on my pants.

I didn't feel safe even as I drove home, clearly shaken. Once I made it inside my apartment, I noticed my hands were still trembling. Who was that following me? What did they want? Did they mean to do me bodily harm?

19

Haviland was planning to move out this weekend back with her actor boyfriend, Trevor, a soap opera B-list actor. They would be moving back to Hollywood Hills, into the house they almost lost to foreclosure. They recently received insurance money for their home invasion robbery. After Haviland and Trevor received the insurance money, they'd caught up their house note and everyone seemed happy.

I didn't know why but something inside of me was suspicious about the story Haviland told regarding the home invasion. My gut just didn't believe that story, but who was it for me to question it. Her insurance had investigated her story, and paid her. So much for my gut churning.

Happily, Haviland had kept her word and was moving out within the month. She was as happy to leave as I was to see her go. She couldn't stand Ben, my pet ferret. "I don't care what you say, Z, that's a rat," she said.

Haviland had also self-appointed herself as the wedding planner for Chica's wedding. Although she and Chica had not exactly hit it off, Chica went along with it because Haviland donated one of her Vera Wang designer wedding gowns that she had worn at one of her three weddings. Truly Hollywood, Haviland had been married three times by the age of thirty. She liked to say, "I like to change my men as much as I like to change my drawers—frequently." She also confided in me that she'd had a boob job, a nose job, and liposuction. Instead of going for thirty-three, she put down she was twenty-four on her acting jobs, which in certain lights she could pass for that age.

"Oh, no, this won't be a ghettofabulous wedding," Haviland declared, reminding me of Whitley from the old show, "Different World." "I'm going to make this wedding look classy and champagne on the beer budget girlfriend has. Tsk, Tsk."

Her words infuriated me. Although she always said she hated her adoptive mother, she always liked to brag about what "her parents" owned. It was through their connections with studio heads that Haviland got her part in *We Are One World.*

I couldn't take her attitude another minute. "Wait a minute, Haviland. I beg to differ with you. Believe it or not, Chica and I were runner ups in a teen beauty pageant. Shirley always made sure we had the best, so don't think just because you grew up in Beverly Hills, you're the only one with good taste."

"Well, excuse me. I'm not trying to be offensive."

"But, you are. In fact, you're very condescending when you talk to Chica. Stop it. Now if you plan to help, do it from your heart, but don't be talking shit because that's my sister."

"Okay, okay." Haviland held her hands up in surrender.

"And another thing that gets on my nerves about you. One minute you act like you had it so hard, then the next minute you're bragging how you were given the best. Now which was it?"

Haviland got quiet. She didn't answer. I guess Haviland knew better than to play with me.

Sometimes I laughed over the extreme differences in my two friends. One was an old friend and one was a new friend. The truth be known, I didn't trust Haviland as far as I could see her.

I guess what we all had in common was that we have had different substance abuse problems and that we wore invisible wounds from all of our birth mothers.

As I came out the shower, my cell phone buzzed. I thought it might be Haviland. When I answered my cell phone, and I heard Romero's soft Hispanic accent, I was surprised.

My heart skipped around my chest as I talked to him, and even I wondered what that was all about. I didn't even know this guy, but he seemed like he was always showing up in my life when I needed him. I wonder if I was catching feelings for him. Then I thought about my bad history with men. "Nah."

"Hey, Z. I got your message."

"Thanks for calling me back."

"You know I didn't mean to sound insensitive that day we were having coffee. Can I make it up to you and take you to dinner?"

I paused for a moment, but I relented. "When?"

"This weekend on Saturday. I've finally got a weekend off."

It was Tuesday, so that gave me time to go shopping. I'd lost all my clothes when I was evicted, and I was slowly tic-tac-toeing and building back up my wardrobe.

I drove down to the Crenshaw Mall and browsed around the women boutiques and dress shops, but I kept getting this uneasy feeling. I kept looking over my shoulder, thinking about the car that followed me. Was that a random car jacking?

I didn't know. As I shopped I felt like someone was watching me, then I shook off that feeling. Maybe I was just getting paranoid.

I finally found an all purpose black dress which could be dressed up or down and picked out a pair of Jimmy Choo shoes.

Driving home, I turned my radio up and start humming to Beyonce's "Irreplaceable." For the first time since Trayvon's death, I felt uplifted. There was something about Romero that I liked. This was a guy who I was feeling and I was sober. It had a whole different feel to it than the men I liked when I was drinking. Maybe my judgment would be better this time.

This was the first time since Trayvon's death that I'd felt a brief moment of joy. But just as suddenly as it came, it left. The dark cloud returned.

I thought about Trayvon. Who were the two men everyone said went up and shot him when he got off the bus? Would I be able to keep my promise to Shirley and to Chica and find the murderer? And what about my safety? Who was driving that car that tried to run me down? Was it because I was poking around in Trayvon's death? And what did F-Loc mean by something strange went down the night of Okamoto's killing?

I felt my palms getting sweaty. I used to be a lot tougher when I was on the force, or at least I thought I was. Maybe I was hiding my fear behind the badge and behind my drinks. Because now without the badge and without bolstering of alcohol, I knew what I truly felt. I was plain scared.

20

The next day, I received a call from Chica who wanted to get together for lunch. "I'll drive down to L.A. How about the Cheesecake Factory in Marina Del Rey?" Chica suggested. "It'll be my treat."

While I was on the force, most of my friends, rather associates, were police officers—mainly men. It was as if I now had to readjust my inner barometer to being around women. It was a whole different world from the "in-your-face, shoot-from-the hip" world of men. For example, if you made an empty gesture of saying, "Let's get together," another officer understood it was just total B.S. But I couldn't say that to my two new women friends; they took it seriously. They held me to the task.

I thought about it. Chica and I had talked more in the past few months than we had since I moved out and left her in Jordan Downs when we were eighteen.

Since we became adults, we'd never really gotten together and did the "sistah girl," chitchat thing, and maybe that would help us since we both were in a twelve-step program. I went to my meetings every day, and although I had a sponsor, it would be nice to have someone who was going through the same thing at the same time.

Maybe this would help me with this spooked feeling I kept getting.

When I arrived, Chica wanted to talk about her wedding too since it was back on. "We've finally reset the date."

"When is it?"

"June twenty-first."

"Great."

"I want you to be my bridesmaid. It's going to be a small ceremony."

"Thanks! You know I got you, girl."

She smiled. We both ordered shrimp scampi and Greek salad. We were sitting on the pier, looking out at the Pacific Ocean lapping gently at the cement posts, and both feeling a sense of calm. This is the first time since Trayvon's murder that she didn't mention him.

"Z . . ." Chica's tone turned serious. "I want to thank you for being there for me with Trayvon." Her eyes misted up, and I was afraid we were going to go back to that desolate place we were when we first got the shocking news of Trayvon's murder. No, we were all getting a little better, one day at a time. I didn't want to fall back into the darkness.

I flagged my hand in dismissal. I took my thumb and pushed it under my chin, in a "Keep your chin up, girl," sign.

I watched as Chica swallowed back her tears. Then, bottom lip trembling, she tried to brighten up and changed the subject. "I just want to know how your investigation into Trayvon's murder is coming along? I appreciate your efforts."

"I don't have any news yet, Chica."

For a moment, her mouth turned down in the corners.

"Don't worry. I believe whoever did this is going to be brought to justice—even if it's street justice."

Tears sprung in her eyes again. "I'm just getting frustrated and I'm mad. You sure you can't move this along faster?"

"I'm doing all I can, Chica. Don't worry."

The waiter came and brought both of our orders, interrupting our moment.

We both began to eat in silence.

"Did I ever tell you how I always admired you, Z?" Chica broke the silence.

I was taken aback. "No, but whatever! Look, girl. I'm just proud of how you've cleaned up." Then teasing, I added, "You clean up real good."

"Thanks! You're doing good, too."

I crossed my arms and tilted my head to the side. "Well, aren't we the motley crew? Two recovering addicts. I guess the pot can't call the kettle black." I paused then spoke from my heart. "You know I'm sorry for how I treated you when you were using. I really can't talk about nobody as bad as I got before I finally got help."

"No, you did the right thing to cut me off. I was treacherous. When I needed a smoke, I would steal from my own grandmother if she'd been alive. I did some scandalous things, I don't care to remember. I was a bottom feeder. At least you never did drugs."

I shook my head as I faced my own moment of truth. "I just can't believe I didn't think what I was using was a drug, but alcohol is a drug too, it's just legal. I really had things twisted."

"Well, if you say so, but Z, you always had something I didn't have."

"What?" I almost scoffed at the idea. For crying out loud, we were both foster kids.

"Confidence. I guess that thing about being a ghetto Mafia princess was true in your case."

"What do you mean?"

"Remember when that gang of girls jumped on me in junior high and you jumped in, kicking ass and taking names?"

"No, you were fighting pretty tough by yourself but it was four of them against the one of you. You know I wasn't going to let them beat up my sister. Anyway, they were just jealous of your hair."

"Well, it's more than just that. I've never held a job and you've had a career—"

"One which I fucked up, don't forget to add that."

"Even so, you went after your dream."

"Well, you were pretty smart in school. I remember you were the best writer in our English class and you know you could quote you some Shakespeare mess."

"Yeah, but I never did anything with my dreams. It's more than just that, Z. You carry yourself like you have a right to be in this world. You act like you can take or leave a man. You know, you're not all desperate acting."

"Wait a minute, sis. I want a man as much as the next sistah, but it seems like I always get it messed up. I really have a problem with giving up my freedom. When I married Rafael, we both were L.A.P.D. and we both had too much ego, so it couldn't work. Now, it's for the best I don't have a man. I'm just doing me.

"Besides, you know the thing about how we're not supposed to get involved with anyone for the first two years of recovery. I think it's for the best for me." Then I thought of Romero. "Now there is this cutie detective, Romero, who I've kind of—I dunno."

Chica didn't say anything. She had her mind on her own problems. She started wringing her hands. "Sometimes I question if I'm marrying Riley for the right reasons."

"What do you mean?" I asked.

"Don't get me wrong. Riley's the best thing that has ever happened to me. But, am I letting Riley rescue me from myself? As fucked up as my life has been, I've always believed in that Cinderella crap. When I was a little girl, I always thought some Prince would ride in and save me."

"I don't get it. It seems like you don't want to be happy. Are you trying to sabotage your relationship? You know we addicts have been known to do that."

Chica shook her head. "I hope I'm not marrying Riley so he can be 'Captain Save a Ho.' I've never held a job in my adult life."

"Now, come on, girl. I've seen this man go through the worse thing in the world with you and stick by your side. He seems to really love you . . . And you know what a cynic I am, so he passes."

Chica slowly broke into a smile. "I guess so. Ever since I was a little girl, it started a pattern. I just have always been a victim and I'm afraid I'm going to screw things up."

"What did Ms. Golden teach us to believe? I'm not your victim—sort of like that program in Texas. Victim no more—right?"

"Okay. Okay." Chica took a deep breath before she went on. "Remember when we studied Shakespeare's *Macbeth* in high school?"

"Yeah."

"I always identified with Lady Macbeth, who is so dang evil."

"Well," I said, "I didn't see her that way. I just saw Lady Macbeth as a lady ahead of her time. Who says women can't be as cold as men?"

Chica didn't answer. "Do you believe that the sins of the father or mother are visited on the children?"

"I don't know. Where are you coming from? You know I'm not that religious so I really can't say. I just think we get generational curses because we keep repeating the same problems our parents had."

Chica glanced around the restaurant and saw that it had emptied out on the pier where we were sitting. "I just wonder if my past is why Trayvon got killed. Y'know there's something I've always wanted to tell you, Z, that I've never told a living soul."

"Uh-huh. What is it?" I absently stabbed my salad with my fork. In fact, my mind had wandered and I was watching a sea gull swoop from the sky, dip down in the ocean, and grab a fish. A school of birds followed him, fighting to take the fish out of his mouth. Their collective bird cries of protest filled the air as they fought for the one fish. *Hmph.* I thought. *Dang. Even dog-eat-dog world in the bird kingdom.*

Meantime, Chica cleared her throat, drawing my attention back to the table. She finally spoke almost in a whisper. "When I was four years old, my mother's boyfriend started molesting me."

"What?" I dropped my fork, and my mouth flew ajar. I was stunned speechless.

"Yes, I was lying to you when I said I was a virgin when we were teenagers. I guess I was in a sense. It had never been my choice to have sex."

My heart started racing in trepidation. "Oh, no, Chica." I reached out and held her hand. "Did he penetrate you?"

"He did it all."

"What do you mean—all?"

"Sucked, fucked, anal, you name it."

"What?" I started fuming inside. Nothing made me angrier than pedophiles posing as boyfriends. "Are you serious? Why didn't you tell your mom?"

"She was too busy getting high herself. She didn't care. You know I used to feel crazy inside. When other little girls were playing with dolls, I was sucking the dick of a grown man."

"Oh, hell naw! Where was your father?" I thought about how my father died trying to protect me.

"He was already serving a life sentence in prison."

"That's awful." I felt hot tears spring to my eyes. I got up and put my arms around Chica, who began weeping softly. "Did you ever tell your mother?"

"I know she knew. I'm just glad the bitch is dead." Chica gritted her teeth.

"Don't say that." Then I felt a cringe of guilt for how I couldn't forgive Venita, so I truly knew how Chica felt. "How about the perp?"

"What's that?"

"The molester."

"I don't know where he is. He left when my mother went to prison, and we were spread all over in different foster homes."

"He's going to get his—if he's still alive." Now, I wish I were still on the P.D. so I could handle this fool.

Chica interrupted my thoughts. "Remember that day when you came home on the first day of the riots?"

"Uh-huh . . ."

"That was my first real time having sex. At least when I sexed Dog Bite, it was my choice and not rape. Anyhow, that's the way I seen it." Chica sniffed, wiping her nose on the back of her hand. "And he gave me a gift. I got pregnant with Trayvon that first month we got together."

I took my napkin and wiped Chica's nose for her. "Now blow," I said, mothering her like I did when we were teenagers. She blew into the napkin, making a loud noise. "I can't believe you never told me before."

"How could I tell you? It's just too nasty. I feel dirty telling you about it even now."

"Well, you shouldn't. The wrong was done to you. You're not at fault." I changed the subject. "Did Shirley know?"

"I think she suspected it because she always had me in counseling, trying to get me to open up as to why I was acting out so."

"Did you ever tell your counselor?"

"Never. I guess I blocked it out, and after I discovered drugs I had the great escape."

"Dang. I guess I was lucky. As many boyfriends as Venita had living up over me, no one ever touched me. I don't know. Strange, that last negro she had my younger brother and sister by, was crazy. It's a good thing he got killed—because no telling what he would have done though. Anyhow, have you ever had therapy?"

"Not since Shirley sent me and I never really opened up. Since I've been in recovery, though, I realize that I've always been a victim ever since that happened. Maybe I should get some therapy."

I slid my arms from around her. I looked Chica directly in the eye. "I'm sorry I judged you so when you were on that crack. I guess it took laying in my own vomit for me to understand. Sometimes this life just gets to be too much and you look for a crutch. Right or wrong, bad or indifferent, this life can be a bitch. Now I see how people wind up on drugs."

Chica attempted to smile and turned to brighter things. "You know I admire how you've never had any children. You've just made much better choices than me."

"Wait a minute. You've got good kids. Yeah, that's right. I didn't have any kids, but I still found a way to flub my life up."

"But you haven't picked a lot of losers like I have." Chica shook her head in regret. "Don't get me wrong—I wouldn't trade nothing for my children. I really want to get them back even more since . . ." Her voice faltered as if she couldn't go on.

"I don't know what I would have done had some grown man been messing with me," I interrupted her, my mind racing back to my past. "I guess Venita's boyfriends always saw how my father came and got me, plus, Mayhem was a stone fool even when he was young and he'd have hurt somebody."

"I wish I had had an older brother, but I was the oldest. In between raising my younger sisters and brothers, I played wife to my mother's boyfriend."

Furious, I pounded my fist into my palm. "I get mad when I think about it. I'm so sorry for you."

"I've tried to get over it in my drug treatment program, but this is the problem. I've never told Riley. Do you think I should tell him?"

"Nah," I said without hesitation. "Some things you can't tell a man. He knows you had five kids, and he knows you were on drugs, that's enough of your business for him to know."

When we parted, I told Chica to call me. "I'll be calling you more," I promised. "We're going to stay more in touch. We need each other, girl."

Chica smiled. "I'm so glad we're back in each other's life—even if it took a tragedy to get us back together. You've always been my best friend."

"You're mine, too. We go way back."

On my drive home, I mulled over what Chica confided in me and I felt myself getting livid all over again. Why were young girls so vulnerable to these sexual predators and why weren't mothers more protective? I thought about all the hookers I'd met on my beat and, most of them said they had been molested when they were minors—and sad to say, most of the abuse took place in their homes.

A few got into the life on their own accord, but for the most part the women were exploited first. Once again,

I was thankful for divine intervention that sent me to Shirley's home.

I almost wished Chica hadn't told me because now I hurt for her. It was not that I excused her behavior over the years, but I better understood and empathized more.

I began to wonder. Was I a victim too, or did I just buy into Miss Golden's "I'm Not Your Victim Program"? Would Chica and I ever be able to escape our crazy childhoods and have a happy life?

21

After I returned home that evening, I received a call from Romero. "How about if I take you to this restaurant in Monterey Park? This place has some of the best Mexican food."

"I'll pick you up, if it's okay?" he asked.

I hesitated before answering. "No, I'll meet you there."

"You sure?"

"Nah, I'm renting from family now and I don't want them all up in my business."

"Are we business as in an item?" Romero's voice sounded teasing.

"We'll see." I chuckled. "Plus, I have something I'd like to show you."

So we decided to meet at seven-thirty that evening outside a Mexican restaurant called Flamingo Pink in Monterey Park.

As I strutted into the restaurant, I noticed how people nodded at Romero with respect. I really should have had him pick me up, but I wanted to feel free to leave when I got ready. Besides, I was on a mission. I wanted to tell him about the threat I'd gotten. I wanted to know if he had any leads that might help me to find Trayvon's killer.

A mariachi band playing maracas filled the air. The walls and ceilings were decorated with sombreros, Congo drums, and nets. The place was crowded with Latinos in the thirty-something crowd.

We were in an area where a plethora of Asian businesses had moved from Chinatown, but I felt rather
safe with Romero. They had every type of gang you
wanted to name in L.A.—Black, Latino, Asian—so you
never could say you were on safe grounds.

Although this area was fairly middle class, I was a
little afraid. Being in San Gabriel Valley reminded me
of when I was mugged in El Barrio during the riots
when I was eighteen. *Fool, you could have been killed*,
I thought. *I must have been out of my freakin' mind. I
guess God does look out for fools and babies.*

No matter how diverse California was, each race of
people and group of immigrants congregated together
in their own little areas.

After we ordered our dinners of chille rellenos, Spanish rice, and refried beans, we ate in silence. All you
could hear was the crunching of our tortilla chips, which
we continually dipped into a hot guacamole and salsa
sauce.

When we were through eating, I broached the subject which had been on my mind.

"I want to show you something," I said.

"What?"

I eased the note with the death threat out my purse
and showed it to Romero

At first, he studied the warning with the cut-out
newspaper letters. A strange look crossed Romero's
face, then ripples of concern replaced it. "Who gave
this to you?"

"I don't know. It was on my windshield about a week
ago. I'm not sure if it's a prank or if it's connected to
Trayvon's death. What do you think?"

I noticed how Romero got quiet, as if he was in deep
thought. At last he said, "I'll look into it."

Then it was as if he completely changed the subject. "Would you like a Margarita—oh, I'm sorry." He held up his hand, as if he had total recall how wasted I was that day he dropped by when I was with Flag. Although I didn't say I was abstaining from alcohol, I thought he knew from the green tea I ordered at Starbucks that I was on some new stuff.

"No, I'm good." I shook both hands in a "I pass," signal.

"Okay. I hope I'm not getting off on the wrong foot with you again. How about if we get up and dance?" Romero pointed to the dance floor on the other side of the bar and the restaurant.

We got up and blended in with the crowd swaying back and forth on the dance floor. At first we began to slowly do the salsa dance. We used slow, languid movements, before we picked up the speed. Once we got wound up, we both did advanced hand flicks like we'd been dancing together for years.

"Where did you learn to dance like this?" Romero whispered in my ear, which surprisingly turned me on.

"I don't know," I cooed. The truth of the matter was I'd always been a good dancer, and it could be my Belizean heritage, but I could Mambo, tango, and do a lot of the Afro Caribbean dances. Like most people from my generation, I liked hip hop, but I was even more drawn to the exotic dances.

The more we swayed, bumped, and grinded, the more aroused I started feeling. The more aroused I got, the more I felt the pull towards sex, which on an intellectual level, I knew would not be good for my psyche or my recovery. Sex clouded my judgment too much. It was just another drug for me. And after this long dry spell, I could jump Romero's bones and tear him up, and I didn't even know him like that. Instinctively, I started backing away from him, once my upper brain took back control of my body.

And what if I was reading more into this than what it was, I pondered. Besides, I had too much on my mind to get involved. My quest for Trayvon's killer crossed my radar, and my libido shut off like a light switch. I visibly backed away from Romero until we finished the dance.

When we finally left the dance floor, Romero took me by the hand and stared deeply into my eyes. "Do you know how many years I've thought about you and dreamed about holding you in my arms?"

"Romero, you don't even know me." I pulled my hand out of his and pushed him gently away, but I could tell I was blushing. I fanned myself. "I could use a cold 7-Up, though."

"Sure." Romero went to the bar and ordered two 7-Ups.

He sat down and looked directly in my eyes. "I know you've been through a lot, yet you're a survivor. You're strong. That's why I like you."

"I don't feel strong right now. I don't want to do any thing right now because I'm too vulnerable."

"What do you mean by anything?" Romero got that amused look I've seen on his face before.

"Anything. Anything stupid. Like take a drink. Like get involved with someone."

Romero held up his hands in resignation. "Look, I've waited all these years. I can wait as long as need be."

"Can I ask you a question?" I asked.

"Shoot."

"Can you follow me home? I'm feeling a little ner-vous—with that letter and all. I don't know why I even came out here tonight."

"Sure."

Romero followed me home on the Santa Monica freeway, and I felt more comfortable. It was after twelve-thirty when I pulled up to my place.

I felt so bad to have Romero drive out of his way from Silver Lake, I invited him up for a cup of coffee. We sat on my futon, and with my legs crossed under me, I sipped my coffee.

"Your place is nice," Romero commented looking around my small unit.

I'd made it comfortable with plants, a nice painting from a garage sale, and my bookshelf was getting filled with Urban literature.

Ben snuck out of his hiding place, and I was surprised at how Romero played with him. Ben even seemed to take to him. He laid on his back, while Romero scratched his stomach, and he got the contented look he'd get whenever I played with him.

We talked to three in the morning.

"You can stay the night," I vaguely recalled saying before I dozed off, with Romero's arms wrapped around me, and for the first time in a long time, I felt safe.

When I woke up, Romero was wide awake, cuddling me and studying me. "I've wanted to wake up and find you in my arms for years. Now it's come true."

I stretched, then looked around remembering where I was. "You better leave before Shirley and the girls get up. She'd never believe there's no monkey business going on."

"Sure." Romero reached over and gave me a deep kiss, morning breath and all, but he pulled away just as quickly. He added, "I'm willing to wait as long as you want, Z. I know this isn't a good time. I want to be there for you. There are some things going on I'm not at liberty to share with you right now, but I'll tell you when I know more."

"What is it?" I perked up, and came fully awake.

"I can't tell you."

"Okay, how about if I invite you to Chica's wedding? You can be my date."

Romero looked excited. "I'd be honored to be your date."

As he pecked me on the lips on his way out the door, I wondered what Romero was holding back.

22

The next day I called L.A. Booking, made sure Collins was still in County Jail, and checked on the visiting hours. I decided, on an impulse, to visit the man responsible for my partner's death. I wondered how I was going to feel. I was not sure what I felt anymore. I did know that being sober made me feel a lot of uncomfortable feelings. I wondered if I were still a police officer, if I would try to take Collins out. I was angry as hell at him, and almost hated I was now a civilian.

After I went through a series of checkpoints, L.A. County Jail looked dreary inside. There were only a few booths for attorneys. I had to wait an hour before I could see him, but I was finally able to see Lawrence Collins.

I flashed my identification, stared at him through the plexy glass window, and watched while he picked up the phone. "Collins, just tell me why?" I gave Collins a dead stare to challenge him to tell the truth. "Why did you kill my partner?"

"So that was you that night? I swear 'fore God and on everything I know and love, I'm innocent. I didn't shoot that police officer."

"Well, the reports say you did."

"Did you ever find out about the ballistic reports? Somebody planted a gun in my house."

"Do you remember what happened that night?"

"All I know is you said you were going to run a criminal check, and when your partner came back, bullets start flying from behind him."

"Are you sure?"

"I'm almost sure the bullets came from behind, because there were bullet holes in our house."

Flabbergasted, I didn't know what to say.

"Look," Lawrence went on, " I only owned a .22. I
knew I was on parole and already had two strikes. I was
clean. I wasn't dealing no more. You saw my kids were
there in the house. I swear they planted those drugs on
me. Please go check the ballistics report. Someone else
did the shooting. I know it was them."

"Them who?"

"The police. There were two other police on the scene."

I didn't remember any back up showing up. "What did
they look like?"

"They both were dark haired. They were wearing
uniforms. Looked like Mexicans, but one could have
been a white boy with dark hair. I'm not sure."

I thought back and tried to remember. All I could remember was shooting back with my Beretta, but I was
not sure if the bullets hit the house.

I decided I would see if I could get an old friend in
the crime lab who might help me.

When I left the jail, twilight had fallen outside. It was
around six-thirty. My mind was spinning with questions. Could the crime site have been tampered with?
Were there other shooters there that night? Then I
recalled something. A voice shouting. What was it the
voice said? "One Time!" Who called out "One Time?"
I'd always assumed it was Lawrence a.k.a. Uncle Pookie.

When I arrived home, I contacted my old friend, Alice Thomas, from the Crime Lab to find out about what
was written up in the Crime Scene lab report.

"You know I'll only do it for you."

"Also, I have one more favor to ask of you, Alice."

"What?"

"I never got my things out of evidence lock-up after my shooting, and I don't know if any one ever claimed my private property lock-up."

Alice hesitated. "I could get in trouble, Z."

"They probably don't need the uniform and belt I was wearing when I got shot. Come on, Alice," I wheedled. "Be a sport."

"All right. I'll see what I can do. How will I get them to you?"

"What time do you get off?"

"Eight."

"I'll meet you at Burger King down the street at eight-fifteen."

While I waited for Alice to get off work, I went back to the address where "Unca Pookie" lived. It took me a while to find the house since I only knew it from memory, and that was in the middle of the night when I went there before. I no longer had the police report, and hopefully, when Alice delivered her package, I'd have some addresses to look at.

Anyhow, the back house looked different in the dim evening light. I hadn't even driven by this spot since I was shot, and it made my stomach flip flop in discomfort—as if my body remembered that it was in mortal danger at this house.

No one appeared to be at home, so I went up to the back house and circled around it. The house still had the same lopsided step. I did notice several bullet holes on each side of the door. I measured the holes with a measuring stick I had in my car. The holes looked like they came from 350 Magnums. How could a bullet hit the house from the outside if Pookie was the shooter? I shot at the house, but I was using a Beretta.

Just as I was leaving, the lady I recalled being named Mimi pulled up in her beat-up Volvo. She had what looked like a six-year-old boy and a three-year-old girl in tow. Now I remembered. These were the kids that were sleeping on the couch that fateful night. "Hey, what are you doing at my house?"

"Hello, Miss Mimi?"

"Yes."

"I'm the police officer who came to place the children that night when Lady Bug was murdered."

"Oh, yeah. I remember you. I'm sorry what happened to you. Are you all right now?"

"I'm fine. Do you remember what happened that night?"

"Okay. You guys said y'all were going to check out Pookie. He was afraid because he knew he had a record, and some outstanding warrants, but he didn't try to shoot nobody for that. He was planning on explaining and seeing if y'all could put the kids in my name 'cause I don't have a record."

"And then what happened?"

"Pookie went to the door, and he hollered out, 'What happened to the other two polices?'"

"All I know is I started hearing something like machine guns going off and we grabbed our babies and hit the floor. Pookie ran and covered us all up with his body."

"Did you see the two police Pookie saw?"

"No, I didn't. But he swears, they were the ones shooting."

"How do you know if he's telling the truth?"

"Things happened so fast, but there's no way Pookie could have done the shooting. We were thinking we were going to get Lady Bug's kids, then the next thing we knew, bullets were flying. We had to get down on the floor to save our own lives. Pookie was laying on top of us to save our lives."

"Did he tell his lawyer?"

"Well, he's had all these court-appointed lawyers and they seem to keep losing his paperwork. I swear on my children's lives, Pookie is innocent."

"That's what I'm trying to find out, Miss. If he is innocent, I'll do all I can to help him."

After I met Alice and got the plastic bag containing my personal affects, the crime lab report, and the police report, I went home and examined the contents. I prayed that the key to Okamoto's safety box was still in my duty belt.

There was nothing remarkable from my bag of clothes. It bothered me seeing the dried blood stains on my police shirt, my bullet proof vest, and undershirt. At the bottom of the bag, I found my duty belt, and was relieved to find the key was still where I'd put it. I had a new problem. I couldn't remember which bank Okamoto told me the safety deposit box was at. I had to think hard.

Now, which bank did Okamoto say his safe deposit box was at? I wondered. So much had happened since then, I truly couldn't remember. "Lord," I prayed, "Please help me to remember."

I went through all the paper work since I couldn't remember the bank's name. I shook my head as I read the reports. First of all, the police report had been tampered with. The times had changed; the type of caliber bullets had been changed. I could see that Lawrence Collins had been royally pencil fucked. None of the facts made sense.

When I got to the bottom of the report, I gasped. The reports were signed by Raymond Norris a.k.a. Flag and Julius Anderson. *What the hell were they doing there?* I wondered. Were they there because of Collins' drug trafficking history? I planned to go interview them, but first I needed to see what was in the safety deposit box. I went online and googled banks in downtown L.A. The name, National Bank, leaped out at me off the screen. I thought that was it, but I wasn't sure.

The next morning I went to the National Bank as soon as they opened. Bingo! This was the bank and I had no problem getting into Okamoto's safe deposit box.

Inside his safe deposit box I found nothing but a CD.

When I made it back home, I fired up my laptop so I could read the disc. Hidden in plain view was a file of Okamoto's called, The Little Black Book. I clicked open the file and all I could say was, "Oh, my God."

The contents from Okamoto's safety box sent pins running down my hairline into my brain. It was as though he was speaking to me from the grave.

"There's important information I want you to get if anything happens to me."

So this was what the key to the safe deposit held. Now I was friggin' scared. I stumbled to the bathroom and threw up, I was so sickened by what I'd read. When I rinsed my face and looked in the mirror, I saw a familiar face looking back at me. It was not my own face. I could now see the resemblance to my mother. I had the same face shape. The same determined chin jutting out.

I picked up the phone, then hesitated, but I went ahead and put in the call. I convinced myself I need to start somewhere. I called my mother. Yes, that was right. I needed my mother. For all she'd put me through, I still needed her.

"Hey."

"Who is it?"

"Mama, it's Z."

23

Since Venita's release, I hadn't visited or called her. I'd refused her calls, and with my trying to stay sober, the first few months, I knew she would have pushed me right over the brink of sobriety and back into the abyss of alcoholism.

Regardless, now I felt a pull to be with my mother. A few good memories were beginning to surface for me. How Venita kept me well dressed by ghetto standards and always clean. My hair was always in the most intricate braided styles. How she always cooked my favorite meals. I guess I'd blocked out those good memories. I still wanted to be angry at her. At the same time, I needed her to give me any information she could as to Mayhem's whereabouts and a current address.

F-Loc had told me to get in touch with Mayhem. He'd hinted that my brother would know more about what was going on. So he might be a lead to information on Trayvon's murder.

Over the years, I'd learned how convicts in the prison system knew just as much, if not more, about what was going on in the outside world, as if they were not locked up. They had eyes and ears everywhere on the street. I also wanted to find out if Venita knew anything about my younger brother's and sister's whereabouts.

I stood in the courtyard of a four-family flat on Hoover, waiting for her to come out after I called her. My mother had been out of prison a minute now, but she was still staying in another half-way house. I guess that was better than being homeless.

Although I didn't intend to speak to her, I had to swallow my pride. And there was something inside of me I hated to admit. I still loved her. After all, she was my mother. And for whatever she did or didn't do, she was the one who could give me the strength to face what I had to do. I needed her strength right now.

"Hi, Zipporah?" My mother's face lit up at the sight of me. She reached over and grabbed me in a bear hug. This time I hugged her back.

When we released each other, we stood there, appraising each other, not as mother and daughter, but as two women. I must admit she looked better. She was only sixteen years older than me and now I could see what a young mother she was. She'd gotten a decent pair of dentures. She wore a decent-enough looking, shoulder-length weave. Although she was not the woman I remembered, she'd cleaned up nicely. I could tell she was clean and sober, too. I remembered my mother being quite the drinker when she was young.

My mother touched my face. "You're beautiful," she said. "Z, you're looking good."

"You too."

Because Venita had a roommate, she couldn't take me to her room, so we sat on a cement bench in a flower garden filled with amaryllises and crocuses in the courtyard. The sky was cerulean blue and it was a cool day for summer. I'd like to see her room, just to see how she was living, but I knew it was against the rules. I knew, though, unless she'd changed, her room would be orderly.

One thing I recalled was that Venita was a neat freak and very clean. Thinking back, all her men said they loved how she kept such an immaculate house in spite of having so many babies.

I really felt like a traitor. I hadn't gone to see her since her release and I just hated I didn't have the Christian ability to forgive. Although it was not all her fault, I never forgot I was the reason our family was broken up. I wondered if she blamed me for what happened. Did I need to make amends with her? But I decided I wasn't ready.

"Can I say something to you, Z?"

"What is it?"

"I'm glad you stopped drinking."

"How did you know?"

"A little birdie told me, but I'm glad. It's time to break the cycle of all that drinking. It sure doesn't help matters."

I knew my mother had always kept up with me through Shirley, so I knew who the 'Little Birdie' was. "I heard that. How 'bout you? Did you ever quit?"

"Years ago. I have over twenty years sobriety, and I haven't touched a drop since I've been out."

"Anyway, what are you doin' with yourself?" I asked.

Venita smiled, looking proud of herself. "I've got a little job at this flower shop. I'm still on parole, but I'm happy. You know I never had a job before."

I thought back. She never worked because her men took care of her, and she got a County check for us kids. "How 'bout you?"

"What about me?"

"What are you doing now?"

"I'm a private investigator."

"Not on the police anymore?"

I started to tell her I was fired, but I couldn't even admit it in my own head.

"No. I like investigations. I like my freedom. I want to find Diggity and Ry-Chee."

Venita didn't say anything, but she smiled at the pos-
siblity of me finding her two youngest children. I guess
Venita was beginning to feel comfortable with me.
"When you gon' give me some grandbabies? You're not
getting any younger."

"Oh, so I can have babies who can end up in foster
care like we did?"

Venita's mouth turned down in the corner and she
looked hurt, which is what I wanted. I wanted her to
hurt like I used to hurt, and like I still hurt. "Okay,
Z, I'm sorry," she said, holding her hands out in an
imploring manner. "I messed up. But you turned out
pretty good."

"No thanks to you."

Venita nodded. "True. What can I say? I'd like to
start building a relationship with you with the time we
have left."

"It's too late, but whatever . . ."

Venita looked crushed again, but I could see some
of the old, proud Venita. She threw her shoulders back
and her head high, as if she said to herself, "Too bad.
Suck it up."

"Do you know where Mayhem is?" I asked.

"No. Y'heard from him?" Venita ventured, on to the
next page already.

I slipped into the vernacular. "Mayhem still banging
with his old self. Still slanging, but I hear he the Man.
In and out of prison. He's getting out the last I heard."

"You have his number?"

"No. I came to see if you knew where he was. Why?"

"I'm just surprised you don't keep up with him. He is
your brother. You used to idolize him when you were a
little girl. Your first words were, 'Who, my big brother,
Dave?' whenever I would fuss about how bad he was.
He's the one who taught you how to handle a gun when
you were only seven or eight."

I tried to remember that time of innocence, that time when I idolized my mother and my older brother. Crazy as it was, I remembered how happy we were as a family. Until I lived with Shirley, I thought it was normal for moms to have live-in uncles, for people to hang out at the house drinking forties and smoking weed all day and night

"I used to say that about Mayhem?" I asked in disbelief.

"Yes, ma'am, you sure did." My mother reminded me of how she would say, "Yes, ma'am," the way someone would say, "I kid you not."

"Well, you're a PI. I'm sure you can locate him—if you want to." Venita sounded hopeful, to know we might reunite.

"I haven't had a chance to look for Rychee and Diggity—but I will."

I thought about it. It seemed like the more effort I put in to trying to find Trayvon's murderer, the more strange stuff kept popping up.

"I don't worry. You'll find them. You were always the strong one, even when you were a little girl. But be careful out there. You know the streets have ears."

With that, Venita reached in her purse and handed me a picture. It was an old black and white with cracks running through it. It looked like a strangely familiar man at the beach, holding a strangely familiar baby.

"Look, I have something for you. This is a picture of you and your father, Butty, when you were a baby."

24

I slipped the picture in my wallet, and decided I'd study the image and think about it later. After I left Venita's, I felt myself getting disturbed. More and more, I felt uneasy.

When I was a drinker, I would take a drink when I started feeling uncomfortable like this, but this time, I fought the urge. To combat the urge, I found an AA meeting in West Los Angeles that met early, so once again, I was able to overcome my desire for a drink.

As if I didn't have enough to be afraid and to be worried about, now I wondered would I be able to stay sober? What trigger might start me back to drinking? Would I be strong enough to resist the urge? I really worried about that. I had resisted taking Antabuse, which would make me sick if I took a drink. I guess it was the equivalent of methadone for a heroin addict. I was hoping to not have to take the drug, but I didn't know if I'd be strong enough to not drink without the help of that little pill.

After the meeting, I was still feeling unsettled. The meeting helped, but I was somewhat depressed. Even so, I pushed forward. I tried to find my brother, May-hem, in this state of distress. I know they say there was "eu-stress" which was good stress, but this was bad stress. I was really caught up.

I was upset over the CD, which had now landed in my care, and could cause me a world of trouble. I pushed that fact into the back of my mind. I needed to move ahead. Maybe Mayhem would have some leads on Trayvon's murder.

I called Chino Prison and found out that Mayhem definitely was released about six weeks earlier. I didn't want to call his Parole officer because it might raise suspicion. It was a long shot, but I needed to try to find him. From the time he joined the Crips when he was about eight, Mayhem had always been one to know what was going on in the streets.

I remembered my brother used to own several houses that he operated out of in Compton. Once when I saw it on a police warrant for search and seizure, I'd checked this one particular address out on my off duty time.

I must admit I was a little leery driving through Compton. With its reputation as a murder capital, who wouldn't be? When I was growing, Compton, where my father had lived, was considered a step up from Jordan Downs. It had been peopled by a lot of homeowners. The truth was, the property had really escalated in value, but recently it was beginning to fall with this housing market crash.

Compton gained its bad reputation in the eighties and nineties when the gangs and drugs began to flood the area.

Today when I drove up to Mayhem's address, I could tell by all the bars on the windows and doors, this was still a hot spot. I'd remembered when Mayhem operated with impunity when I was on the force, but I had to turn my head the other way. Besides, Compton wasn't in our jurisdiction at the time I was a cop.

Eventually, everything must have caught up with Mayhem. The fact that he only served eighteen months made me think he must have had a really good set of lawyers, or he would have served more time than that.

I took a deep breath as I stepped out my car. I slowly walked up to the door and knocked. I held my breath and waited. I listened as multiple locks unlatched with a snapping noise of several locks.

"What do you want?" a buffed guy, who was hefty and resembled Michael Clarke Duncan, barked. I stepped inside this iron-barred house in Compton, and a coldness rippled through me. A sense of pure evil resided in these walls.

"I'm looking for Mayhem. I'm his sister, Z." Three goons checked me before they let me pass the front foyer.

"Big Homie," the Michael Clarke Duncan look-alike announced, "some young lady saying she's your sister is here. Says her name is Z."

As I waited, I glanced around and noticed they had a fish tank that covered the entire wall in what was supposedly a living room. There was no furniture in this room, and no place to sit down, but I didn't want to sit anyhow. I studied the fish tank, which was filled with devilfish, which I understood were poisonous. I hated to think what this fish tank was used for. I'd heard that some dealers used devilfish to poison snitches or anyone who crossed them.

"Who the hell are you?" a deep male voice snapped, suspiciously.

I almost jumped in my skin at this male voice, but I was insulted he didn't remember me. I looked up at Mayhem. "David," I called him by his government name, "this is your lil' sister, Zipporah, aka Z. I know it's been a long time, but don't tell me you've forgotten about me. Don't you remember I was the one who used to follow you around the projects? The one who used to say, 'Who Dave, Mama?' to Venita, when she would say how bad you were."

For a moment, Mayhem's implacable features froze like a mask. Then slowly, a glimmer of recognition flashed in his face.

"What? My li'l sis?" I could see a smile start rising in his face. "Aw, snap. Z, is that you?"

Who do you think I am? I wanted to say, but I knew he was not a person to be joked with. "In the flesh."

"What's crack-a-lacking? Babygirl, you all grown up." Mayhem lifted me off my feet in excitement, and I had to remind myself that he was my brother and I'd loved him dearly as a child. I had to separate the man from the myth and ignore the fact his reputation preceded him.

"Come on in my office," he said. I followed my brother into what was probably a bedroom, but it now only had a desk and a chair in it. He closed the door behind us—I guess for privacy. Something made me think this chair was more of a hot seat for people who stole Mayhem's products.

Inside, I trembled, but I held my hands still. I hoped Mayhem couldn't pick up on my fear. I wasn't afraid of the boy I remembered, but I was afraid of the man he'd become.

I noticed Mayhem was now called Big Homie because he was so buff. His upper arms possessed corded muscles. I hadn't seen him since we were in our late teens, and although he looked older, he'd aged well. His pecan skin was as smooth as butter cream, he sported a bald head, and his nails were clean. His slacks were neatly creased, and although he didn't wear any bling, like he did when I last saw him, he carried himself in a regal manner. Just looking at the influence he exerted over the other men, he could easily have been the president of a corporation if he'd been born in a different time and place.

"Dang. How did you get so big?" I asked, trying to act relaxed in front of my brother, the killer.

"Exercising. Pumping iron." He bent his elbow and let me see him flex his muscles.

"I thought they stopped allowing all that pumping iron in the joint."

"Well, some of us had our own private equipment, y'know what I mean." He raised his eyebrow in a conspiratorial fashion.

I guess so with Mayhem being a drug kingpin, he probably had more freedom and more access to outside services than the average inmate.

"Excuse my place," he said, fanning his hand around the sparsely furnished house. "I used to have a mansion in Beverly Hills, but the Feds confiscated all my shit. I'm a be all right though. I had some money put away. Anyhow, I'm getting back on my feet, and I'm on parole, so I have to be on the low-low. You know what I mean. I'm gon' to have all that stuff back and more in a minute."

I didn't say anything. How could I condone drug trafficking, as screwed up as it had made our lives and so many of our neighbors—our whole community? But, at the same time, I acted nonjudgmental since I liked breathing in and out—yes, I loved this thing called life. And I never forgot one thing. My brother, Mayhem, was a killer. He could be smiling at you one minute and take you out the next.

"Do you have any little nieces or nephews for me?" Mayhem asked me.

"Nah." I let out a "Whew!" and almost a Thank goodness sigh.

"It's probably for the best." Mayhem looked stern. "I'm glad you didn't grow up in the projects with all those chuckleheads running around. I probably would have had to hurt someone over you as fine as you are. But I'm proud you ain't got a bunch of crumb snatchers trailing behind you. Y'know, Venita started having babies at fourteen."

I decided to lighten the mood and hit upon a more pleasant subject. "How about you?" I asked. "Married? Any kids?"

"Hell nah, I ain't married. I got a wifey, though. Three different baby mamas—all boys. They ain't nothing but trouble."

"So I'm an auntie. I've got to meet my nephews."

"Yeah, you should meet those little thuglets." Mayhem said this with pride.

Oh, no, another generation of Crips.

Without warning, Mayhem switched horses in the middle of the stream. "Z, do you remember how I taught you how to shoot when you were about seven?"

I had squashed that memory with so many others, until Venita mentioned it. "Yeah." Now I could see how I never had any problem "qualifying" when I would go to the rifle range while with the Department, or when I was in the Police Academy. I was quite the marksman, or should I say *woman.*

"Have you seen Venita?" I asked.

"Naw. I heard she's out now."

"Yeah, she is. I saw her the other day."

"How she look?"

"Much better than when she first got out. How's Big Dave?"

Since we had different fathers, I never did keep up with Mayhem's father. I was just being cordial. All I know was we had the same mother, came out the same womb, and that was all that counted. It was "Mama's baby, Daddy's maybe," the way I saw it. I'd just lucked up that I'd had a better father than Mayhem.

"Fuck that nigga. He still shootin' heroin in his arm."
His mouth tightened into a stubborn line of resent-
ment.

"I'm sorry to hear that."

"Ain't nothing worse than an old ass junkie." Mayhem sucked his teeth in disgust. "He the reason I ain't
never touched none of that shit . . . But if people want
to use the shit, somebody gotta make the money. Might
as well be me." He flashed a wicked grin, which made
me think of Satan and I almost showed my fear, but I
never forgot the first law of the jungle. Show no fear.

I disagreed with Mayhem, but I knew he was not a
person you could disagree with him, so I changed the
subject. "You know I'm trying to find Diggity and Ry-
chee."

Mayhem averted his gaze, as if it pained him to remember our younger siblings. Now it was his turn to
change the subject. "Anyhow, I heard you were five-oh
for a long time."

"Yeah. Not anymore."

"I hope you got you a piece and keep it on you."

"Why?"

"Just can't be too careful. You being a former cop
and all." Obviously, he'd kept up with me through the
street grapevine and the prison grapevine.

"You knew I was on the force?"

"Yeah. I knew it the whole time. I have my ways of
knowing things. I figured that's why you never came
and talked to me, but that's cool. You had to do what
you had to do."

"Well, I'm here now."

"Yeah, I heard about that shit that went down."

"Which one?" Shit, I stayed in so much trouble with
that drinking, I didn't know which incident he was talking about.

"The shooting. I'm sorry to hear about it. From what I've heard, you were a straight cop."

I saw my chance to leap in with my original intention. "That's why I came to you. I never tried to put any shit in the game, and I don't know of anyone who would try to be getting back at me. That's why I'm trying to find information on who killed my nephew, Trayvon."

"I thought you didn't know where Diggity and Rychee is. How you an auntie if you don't know my kids?"

"My foster sister, Chica, has five, well had five, now she has four. We were raised together in the same foster home."

"Oh, okay. But look, li'l niggas get smoked all the time in the hood. Don't nobody even give a fuck who did it. That's just how it is."

"Well, I do care." I felt my blood pressure rising, I was so furious. I knew how, because it happened so frequently, many times the murder of black boys or men didn't even make the newspaper or TV news. "Trayvon was family to me. I'm trying to find his murderer."

"They got so many unsolved murders for us, they don't care, sis. Just one less nigga as far as they're concerned. It's a war out here."

"Well, I care. Can you help? Do you know anything?"

Mayhem was silent for a while. When he spoke up, his voice sounded cryptic. "Peep this. This thing is bigger than you know, lil' sis. Be careful. Word is that some Narcs got in hock for a lot of drugs with the Crips, and the Mexican Mafia, playing both ends against the middle. I don't know who these pigs are because they use street names. They go by L and M like those old cigarettes. I was on lock down when this shit went down, so they never bought or sold to me. "

"Where are they now?"

"They done went ghost on a nigga. No one has seen them lately. See, their cover got blown."

"Does anyone know who they are?"

"Those that knew done got wasted or are in witness protection programs one."

"Okay, but what has that got to do with Trayvon's murder?"

"I don't know, Sis. All I know is your partner knew something on them, and he was getting ready to turn state's evidence on whoever it was. He was an honest cop, like that Jake dude in *Training Day*. That's why he got wasted. I hear they shot you, too. You all right? You sure you safe?"

"I'm fine now."

"Yeah. Y'know I just got out and just found this out myself. I don't now if it was L and M, there's so many crooked pigs out there. I don't know who did it yet, but when I find out who shot my baby sister, I'm gonna take care of it."

Oh, shit, I thought. *This is trouble.* I got through the rest of our visit without showing my fear. We exchanged cell phone numbers and hugged each other.

"Be careful, Baby sis," Mayhem said, walking me to my car.

I didn't breathe deeply until I was out of Compton. You talking about relieved. I knew he was my brother, but I hoped I didn't have to see him anytime too soon.

The pieces were beginning to come together for me. It was bad enough the crime lab report had been tampered with, and the bullets taken from Okamoto's body had somehow mysteriously disappeared. But some of those names on the CD were not code names. Each allegation, from money laundering to drug racketeering to murder, to pandering of women, and all the perpetrators were law officers, top brass, or politicians.

Some of them were cases I'd heard about when I was on the force, or crimes I'd heard on the radio, but many I hadn't heard of. But was Okamoto's murder related to the information on the CD? Who could have been the shooter? It could have been anyone. From what I'd read of the police record, the place was surrounded by law enforcement before they took me off to UCLA when I got shot.

I went on line and checked old newspapers and found each crime named had a date. Some of the crimes were not even reported in the media. I remembered the large quantity of confiscated drugs which had come up missing at the Police Central locker. But one of the names on the list was named L who was—Raymond Norris aka Flag.

Was this what Okamoto was planning on telling me? What was I going to do?

25

After my visit with Mayhem, I fell into a state of turmoil, for that night. I couldn't sleep. I was twisted up all inside. Because I was uncomfortable, I started jonesing for a drink again. I also wanted to take a drink because this searching for Trayvon's killer was really getting next to me. I knew I had to do something, or I'd give in to my addiction.

I called my sponsor, Joyce.

"Joyce, I need help. Can I come over to the program?"

She agreed. "I hear the tension in your voice. Are you all right, Zipporah?"

"No, I'm afraid I'll take a drink." I paused. "This thing is getting harder each day."

I wished I had kept a sponsor when I was on the force and had gone to AA. I'd thought about the coping techniques Joyce taught us while we were in rehab. She was good with using imagery and visualization.

It just seemed that nothing was working anymore. I'd tried all of what I remembered from her techniques that helped me cope with stress, but now that I was sober, none of these things seemed to be working.

I couldn't wait until I sat in Joyce's office on her sofa and closed my eyes, listening to her calming voice.

"See yourself standing on top of a mountain. You're in your special place. Surround yourself with all your loved ones. This is where you go to heal."

I tried to put myself on that mountaintop, but I was too stressed out. It was not working like it did when I was a child or when I was an adolescent. I tried to imagine my loved ones, but instead of visualizing a simple nuclear family unit, I saw several families together with jagged edges. First, there was Venita, and my three half-siblings, Mayhem, Diggity and Rychee. Then there' was Shirley, Chill, Chica, and Chica's surviving children, Malibu, Charisma, Soledad, and Brooklyn.

When I opened my eyes at the end of the session, I didn't feel any better. I hadn't even scratched the surface of what was going on with me. My sponsor was blonde and had blue eyes and it was embarrassing to even try to explain the family dynamics and dysfunction, which I grew up in. I left her office, feeling discouraged. I guess this was some 'family work,' as she called it, that I was going to have to put in myself.

That evening, when I made it back to my apartment, I kept staring at the picture of me with my daddy when I was about a year old. My thick head of baby hair had fallen out and I was baldheaded as an egg, but I looked a lot like my father. Same eyes. Same nose. Same forehead.

I dozed off with Ben curled at my feet. I had the same recurring dream, about my daddy sitting up with the bullet hole in his chest, talking to me. But this dream felt real.

"Go back, Zipporah," he said, "and you will get the truth. The truth will set you free."

I sat straight up in my bed, dripping in sweat and heart palpitating so loud I could hear it in the room. I had to go back, but I needed to sort through what I could remember.

"Certain things are meant to be," Venita used to say. According to my mother, the Santa Ana winds blowing in trouble was one of those things. I never forgot how my mother, looking out the door, watching leaves gust and pirouette in the rising wind, used to twist her mouth from side to side and shake her head. Grunting, she'd add, "A bad omen sure as my name is Venita I Love Jordan De la Croix."

Perhaps that's why when she met Strange, she didn't see the wind at his back. She only noticed how he could talk to birds and that he had a parrot on his left shoulder. I didn't have any pictures of them, but I still had a picture in my mind and in those images they were both young.

Just say our lives changed when Strange came to live with us in 1980. With what happened the fall of '83, the Santa Anas had to be blowing something fierce that year. Afterwards, the world became strangely off-color and off-key. Even the leaves on the oak trees in L.A., which, contrary to belief, do turn amber, maroon, and cardamom in fall, gained a sinister look. Underneath the smell of jacaranda, oleander and eucalyptus prowled the smell of death. Yesterday, as I contemplated this enigma, I had no idea it would be an omen.

When I was growing up, my mother used to get depressed every December. That was the month the man she was living with left her when she was eight months pregnant with me because he heard that Venita wasn't carrying his baby. True enough, when I was born, the rumors turned out to be true. Dave came back for a minute, but left her as soon as he saw me. He was light-skinned with kinky red hair, and I was dark-skinned with what they called "jet-black, good hair." Venita was a red-boned beauty, as they called them back in the day.

I'd been conceived by a man unknown at the time, but later my biological father claimed me.

Just from what I pieced together, Venita met my Belizean father, Buddy, pronounced Butty, with a harsh tee sound, when she was living with Mayhem's father, Big Dave. She was slipping around seeing my father, who wasn't a Crip, and who was a working stiff. Well, she accidentally got knocked up with me.

For a short time, my father, Butty, lived with Venita, but she cheated on him, too.

When I was little, my mother always said my real father was no good. However, as I became older, I learned from Butty that my mother got pregnant by another man when he lived with her, and that's why he left her. Anyhow, this baby died at childbirth. Later, he married, but he vowed to always take care of me. I'm telling you, Venita had been as scandalous as a man when she was young. She believed in keeping what people in the hood called "a spare tire"—a man on the side.

All through the years, though, my mother had a live-in boyfriend, but when she got with Strange, Diggity's and Rychee's father, she was a little older (early twenties) by ghetto standards, and a little more desperate. After all, who did she think would want her with two kids with two different daddies?

Now as rough as Venita was, she allowed Strange to beat her. I knew it was "allowed" because I'd seen her whip a police's ass once before six other cops restrained her.

Anyhow, Venita was pregnant with Ry-chee when the problem that divided our family happened.

Memories start flooding back to me as I went back to sleep and revisited the past, which I'd repressed, like a bad dream.

***

Memories start flooding back to me as I went back to sleep and revisited the past, which I'd repressed, like a bad dream.

My mother, who had never been married, was about four months pregnant, carrying Rychee, with Diggity barely a toddling year old infant, when Strange started beating the crap out of her in their bedroom one night. I was sleep, but the banging noises and loud screams woke me up. I ran to their room and opened their bedroom door, stood in the doorway, and yelled, "Stop! Leave my mama alone!"

Strange, with his crazy self, was holding an iron over Venita's face, threatening to bash her head in. As soon as he heard my voice, he climbed off Venita. He stood up and turned around like someone in a slow motion film towards me. He glared at me, eyes shining fox fire red like the devil's.

"I'm a call my daddy. Get yo' hands off my mama!" I shouted again, my hands placed on what Black folks used to call 'imaginary hips' on pre-adolescent girls, just the way I'd seen Venita do all the time.

"Oh, yeah. Tell him this."

With that, Strange flashed opened his robe and exposed his penis, which oddly was standing out like a pole. This fool had an erection like he was getting off, just beating up on my mama, which I didn't understand at the time. But I knew something was wrong with this whole picture. Something evil. Underneath it all, on a primitive level, I knew that I had been violated.

"Yeah, what?" Strange taunted. "What? Now you grown now?" he added, as if he wanted to screw me.

I turned and ran to the phone and called my father. "Daddy, Strange is over here beating up on Mama and he just showed me his ding-a-ling when I told him to stop."

Well, my father, who used to pick me up on weekends, and who always had financially supported me, started cursing in Spanish. He didn't live that far away and he was at our front door in about ten minutes, it seemed. He'd obviously grabbed his gun and came over ready to shoot Strange.

When I answered the door, my father grabbed me up in his arms. "Did he touch you, babygirl?" he demanded.

"No," I whimpered.

My father put me back down on the floor, pushed past me, cursing in Spanish. He rushed to the bedroom, lunged at Strange and grabbed him up off Venita. See Strange was still beating on Venita when my daddy arrived. After that, the two men got to tussling. Venita jumped on Strange's back, trying to help my father fight Strange.But somehow, Strange wrestled control of the gun from Butty and shot my father in the chest. My father slumped over, then fell backwards to the floor.

My daddy laid there, eyes wide open, a bloody hole in the middle of his chest. As soon as I saw the blood, I started screaming at the top of my lungs.

Time seemed to stop. What happened after that proceeded in slow motion.

From out of nowhere, another loud blast penetrated the room. Strange was standing with his arm raised to hit Venita again, but he stopped, his fist raised in mid-air, and grabbed his chest. He looked down, as if he was surprised to see the big hole in his chest. He fell to his face. In the doorway, Mayhem stood holding a smoking gun.

With that, I sat up, wide awake. It all came rushing back to me.

For years, everything had been mixed up and murky in my mind. I always thought it was my mother who shot Strange, but for the first time, I faced a memory I had buried deep inside my heart. It was ten-year-old Mayhem who pulled out a gun and shot and killed Strange!

For the first time, I realized something. My mother had taken the blame and had done time to save Mayhem's ass . . . A mother's love? I didn't know. I didn't even know anything anymore.

Could I ever talk to them about this? Or was this a family secret? I guess it was because after all these years, no one had ever talked about it. Now, I had to keep this secret myself because it would cause too much mess to stir up the truth. At the time, I didn't know what the repercussions would be from that one phone call. But this I did know now. When I was nine years old, I wiped out my entire family in just one phone call.

Because of my father's subsequent death and my mother's resulting imprisonment, I broke up our family. I figuratively killed our whole family because we all wound up in different placements and a part of us, as we knew ourselves, died, never to be replaced.

Now I was a virtual stranger to my oldest brother Mayhem, and had no idea where my younger two siblings, Diggity and Ry-chee, were in this world. I knew I was a child at the time and I couldn't be held responsible for the choices made by the adults in my life, but I still would always regret breaking up our family, as dysfunctional as it was. Because who was to say that the state made a better parent? Mayhem had been in a dozen group homes before he ran away one final time when he was about thirteen. From there, the Crips became his father until he became a leader.

I lucked up on one good foster home, but how did Diggity and Ry-chee fare? The foster homes I visited them in had been average, but then they were adopted as part of some campaign to adopt older black children and it was a closed adoption. Now I didn't know what had become of them. Were they still even in California?

For this reason, all I knew was that night would haunt me the rest of my life.

26

The next day, as I awakened, I felt a deep darkness
inside my soul, but there was also a light. In a crazy
way, I was glad to know my mother was not a killer—at
least not in this case. Maybe this would restore some of
my faith in the goodness of mankind.

I was glad that I finally had accepted the truth about
what happened that night, but I had a more pressing
concern now. I couldn't just sit and relish my father's
picture and think about what his death had meant to
and for me.

Right now, I wanted to talk to my brother, Mayhem.
I didn't know what I'd say to him; I just wanted to
see him again. This surprised me because when I saw
him before, I thought I wouldn't care if we didn't see
each other anymore, or at least any time soon. Now, I
wanted to feel a connection to someone who went back
to that fateful night with me, someone who had lived
through it with me.

I thought about calling Venita and confronting her
with what I knew, but then I thought, *What's the point?*

She might even deny it. She did her time and she
didn't seem to be complaining about it. Maybe that was
a can of worms I didn't want to open.

When I dialed Mayhem's number, my hands were
shaking.

"Hey, sis," Mayhem answered on the second ring.

"Mayhem, I'd like to see you again—today, if possible?"

Mayhem hesitated. I could hear a pain in his voice. "Well, lemme see. I've got to rearrange a couple of meetings, but anything for you, sis."

Yes, I guess so. You killed for me when I was a child. . . . But you were a child, too.

"How about at Dock Weiler?" I asked, knowing this beach was near Compton. All he'd have to do is go straight out Rosecrans Street until it ended at Pacific Coast Highway.

"What time?"

"Two o'clock okay with you?"

"Fine. What'll you be driving?"

"I'll be in a blue Toyota Corolla. How about you?"

"A black Benz."

When I sat across the road from the ocean, I felt myself calming down. I drove to Doc Weiler Beach early, just so I could gather my thoughts.

I watched as the surf lapped against the shoreline and I got a little clarity. There was only one thing I knew for sure. Mayhem was my brother and I had lost too many years. I still didn't know what I was going to say to him. This was the Mayhem no one knew. Everyone just saw him as *Big Homie* or *The Man.* His rap sheet saw him as a criminal. They didn't know that this was a man who had been taking care of himself since he was ten years old, a man who killed for his younger sister's honor in a society which didn't care about its women.

I jumped when someone tapped on the window.

I looked up and saw Mayhem. I saw his goons standing nearby. He tipped his hand to them that it was okay and he climbed in my bucket with me.

"Sis, what is it? You sounded serious."

I paused. There was no sense in us talking about the murder since it was too painful.

"Mayhem, I just wanted to tell you I love you, big bro."

"Love you too, sis."

We sat there, quietly, not saying a word for about five minutes.

Mayhem finally shifted in his seat and opened the door. "I guess I gotta get on and handle my business."

"Okay."

"Sis, please be careful. I worry about you. If you need anything, call me."

I reached over, gave him a hug, and kissed him on the cheek.

Mayhem slowly hugged me back. "Take care of yourself, baby sis."

27

As I drove away from the beach, I realized how if Mayhem and I would have been raised together, we could sit and talk about what happened. Maybe not. In our shorthand way of communicating, he knew I understood what he'd done for me. Well, we certainly weren't the *Brady Bunch*.

Just as I was approaching LaCienega and Rodeo, a large SUV bulldozed towards me and almost hit me head on. The vehicle would have hit me, if I hadn't whipped my steering wheel to the right and pulled on to the shoulder of the road.

Once I got my bearings, I looked over my shoulder. Was that an accident or on purpose near-miss? I was really getting afraid now. I was going to have to take action fast.

I finally realized something I'd been trying not to face. My life was in danger, and so could the lives of my family if I continued to stay here at Shirley's. Who could I turn to? I didn't want to call Mayhem back, or it would just create more murders. It wouldn't be nothing but a word for my fool ass brother to order hits, but who would he have killed? Who shot Okamoto, if it wasn't Pookie? Who shot Trayvon? Even if Mayhem knew who did it, he'd get involved and I didn't want that, either.

No, I wanted the court system to handle Okamoto's and Trayvon's murder. This was something that could get bloody if Mayhem got involved.

I decided to call Romero. Yesterday, I'd made copies of the CD, and I placed them in another safe deposit box. Once I knew who I could trust, I would hand them over to the proper authorities. I didn't know if I could trust Romero like that yet.

"I need your help," I said. I explained all the strange occurrences. "I don't want to endanger my family."

"Why don't you come and stay with me—under protective custody, strictly business—until we get some of these things cleared up. We'll send the police to check your family's house at night."

"Thanks!" I wrote down his address, then hung up, hands trembling.

I gathered my wits together and rushed over to Shirley's house. "Moochie, I'm going to have to go underground—just for a minute." I hesitated before I continued. "It's part of my investigation on Trayvon's murder." I didn't add that it seemed as though Trayvon's murderer or murderers were stalking me, and might come after them if I continued to stay with them.

Shirley looked concerned, but her mind was not really on what I was saying. Lately, she was consumed with Daddy Chill. Last week, Shirley told me the doctor recently diagnosed him with dementia. It's as though Shirley had transformed from being fed-up to a concerned, care-giving wife with an ailing husband.

Oh, well. I guess the divorce was off again, which I was happy about that. Now the wedding would feel like family for Chica and me. After all, Shirley and Chill had been our stand-in parents for over the past twenty years.

Just like Trayvon's death took Shirley's mind off her own issues regarding her wanting a divorce, now she was there for Chill . . . just because. Maybe this was what floated Shirley's boat. Taking care of people.

I knew I was only on the outside looking in and I knew I only had a bird's-eye view as to what went on between two longtime married people, but all I could say was love was some crazy shit. I didn't think I'd ever been in it. Thank God. That was too much love in the world for me.

Shirley had been driving Daddy Chill back and forth to doctor visits, and setting up home nurse visits for him. She waved her hand, absently, dismissing me. "Be careful. I guess you know best how to handle this investigation."

Back at my apartment, I called Chica.

"Any news about Trayvon's killer yet?" Chica asked. She sounded hopeful.

"Chica, I'm going to have to go underground for a minute. Someone's been following me and I don't want them to mess with the fam."

"I'm getting tired of waiting on some news about Trayvon. I bet you just want to go off and be with that Romero. I'm sick of you. That's all right." She slammed the phone down in my face.

Chica and I had argued before when we were teens, but this was the first time she'd ever really gone off on me. I was too upset and too nervous to worry about Chica right now. I'd explain everything to her later. I decided I would call her once I got settled.

I threw a few essential items, with inter-changeable tops and jeans, into an overnight bag, which was attached to rollers. I also packed a couple of wigs, a floppy hat, and large shades. I carefully packed a copy of the CD into a padded envelope, then hid it in a secret compartment in my lap top carrier. I grabbed my lap top, and bags, then headed over to Silver Lake, which was in a hilly area east of Hollywood.

When I pulled up in front of his home, I didn't see his car. I was about to pick up my cell phone and call Romero, but my phone rang. It was six in the evening.

"I got tied up on a case, Z," he said, "but the key is in the planter on the right side of my porch."

I dug through the potted geranium and found a silver key about a half inch buried in the dirt. I let myself inside, looked around at Romero's definite alpha-male decorated house, with its various brown and beige earth tones, and plopped down on the leather sofa. I noticed a house phone, and other than a cart of OJ in the refrigerator when I wanted to get something to drink, it didn't look like anyone else lived there—a real bachelor's pad.

I looked out in his backyard and was surprised to see an in-ground swimming pool.

I called Shirley and let her know I was safe. "I'll be underground for a while, so unless it's an emergency, don't call. You can leave all messages on my cell phone."

I called Chica, and she hung up in my face. I shook my head. What was that all about? I wondered. The police hadn't made any progress in finding Trayvon's murder, and I was doing the best I could. I just didn't know all that digging up would stir up so much trouble. The next thing I knew, I dozed off.

"Hey, sleepy head." I woke up and Romero was standing before me, looking really happy to see me. "Hey, I bought Chinese food. Hungry?"

"Sure 'nuff!" I yawned and got in a yoga-type stretch. I hadn't slept that deeply in a while. For the first time in a minute, I was able to sleep without being afraid.

After we finished eating a spread of moo goo gai pan and fried rice, we sat on Romero's redwood deck, which faced the Santa Gabriel Mountains, and just relaxed. It was twilight and a purple haze settled over the mountains in the evening, and the sight was absolutely breathtaking. The twitter of birds singing decorated the air. Sequoias and oak trees wrapped around his back yard. The scenery was so serene and peaceful that something seemed missing. Then I realized it was the absence of blaring police sirens and helicopters.

"Do you think I'll have to stay here long? I've got to get back to my investigation on Trayvon."

"Well, we're closing in on some leads. The main thing is you need to stay out of harm's way right now. We have detectives on Trayvon's case."

"Do you think my poking around is what made the killer come after me?"

"Could be. Well, you stay here until we make an arrest. We have some leads that I think will pay off."

I guess to take my mind off how scared I was, Romero changed the subject. He brought up the issue of relationships.

"Z, have you ever been in love before?"

"Why do you ask?"

"You just seem kind of in a shell. Like you don't let people get too close to you."

"People or men?"

"Okay, men." Romero threw his head back and let out a delicious-sounding guffaw.

"Like I said, I've been married before. Just put it this way. Being an officer didn't quite add to my "marriage-ability" factor. It didn't help that my husband was on the force too. Our egos were too big, and somebody was about to get hurt up in that mug."

Romero chuckled. "I know what you mean. Are you seeing anyone now?"

"Nah!" I turn to Romero. "How about you?"

"No. Work is my woman."

"How long were you married?"

Romero heaved a sigh before he answered. "Five years. It wouldn't have lasted that long if it weren't for my little girl."

I tried to hide my shock. "You have a child?"

"Yes, I do. She's four. Her name is Bianca. Does it make a difference to you?"

"Not really." I shrugged. "I've dated men with children before, but if you must know, I'm not a kiddy person. Why didn't you tell me before now?"

"It just never came up. Plus, I don't introduce my daughter to just anyone."

"Am I just anyone?"

"No. Under different circumstances, you could be someone special."

"What do you mean?"

"Hey, why don't you give me a chance?"

"I thought we were going to keep this platonic."

"We are."

"You know what they say about relationships based on intense experiences or relationships that start in a crisis?" I teased.

"What do they say?"

"They never work."

"Okay, I've got a few days off. How about, instead of you staying cooped up here, worrying, let's run up to Santa Barbara and hit the missions? You can wear a wig and sunglasses, but we just need to relax for a minute."

We sat on the deck until late that night, just talking. I smelled the redolent smell of jasmine in his back yard and it really soothed the senses.

"There's the Big Dipper," Romero said, pointing to the sky. "On the other side is the Little Dipper."

"Ooo-wow," I said when I stared up at the alignment of the stars. I never noticed these when I was in the city.

"Do you think about your partner—what was his name?" Romero asked, his question seemingly coming out of nowhere.

I choked up. I hadn't really talked about Okamoto to anyone since I talked to the Department's shrink right after I was fired.

"Okamoto. Yes, I think about him, but since I got into AA, I think about him in terms of the serenity prayer."

We both quoted in unison:

God, grant me the serenity
To accept the things I cannot change;
Courage to change the things I can;
And wisdom to know the difference.

"Did you ever get counseling regarding his death?" Romero probed.

A side of me wanted to clam up, but he sounded so sincerely concerned, I admitted, "No. What counseling I did get didn't help because I was too messed up at the time."

"What kind of guy was Okamoto?"

"He was straight. He was just good people."

"I understand you two were really close."

"I guess we were as close as you could expect two cops from two sides of the racial divide to be."

"No, people say you two spent a lot of time together."

"Wait a minute. Have you been snooping into my business?"

"No, I just feel bad that things went down the way they did—you losing your job and all, and losing your friend—that is, if Okamoto and you were good friends."

"Well, number one, I was the one drinking, so I can't blame anyone but myself. I would give anything to get back that night, but you know that thing about we get no do-overs in life. And in case you heard that we were lovers, we weren't, which that's none of your business anyhow. "

I couldn't see Romero's face in the dark, but his voice sounded cool, measured. "I'm glad to know that. Sometimes sex gets into the picture and messes up our objectivity in this job."

"Well, we didn't have it like that. We were partners—and friends. Platonic friends." I stood up. "I think I'm ready to go to bed. Where can I sleep?"

"You can have my bed. I changed the sheets this morning so they're fresh. I'll take the couch."

The next morning I tried to make calls to see what I could find out while I was underground. I called Alice. She whispered in the phone, "Z, I can't help you anymore. They've been checking on me. I'm on probation."

I asked could I have her cell phone number since she couldn't talk on the business line. When she complied, I called her when she was on her break. I wanted to ask her to scan or get a list of all the officers and supervisors who were present the night of my shooting. I knew it was a long shot, but I had to see if I could narrow down who shot me and killed Okamoto.

Unfortunately, when I called Alice back, she didn't answer. I took that as a 'no.' I was going to have to go and face her to get that information.

While I was waiting, I found out Romero had a collection of movies I liked and some I was not familiar with.

One, MS-13, the Mara Salvatrucha gang. The Gang was set up in the 1980s by Salvadoran immigrants in the city's Pico-Union neighborhood. To pass time, I read up on them online. I wondered if they were responsible for Trayvon's death. I made a note to look into them.

He also had DVDs's of *The Godfather, Scarface, Rocky,* and *Training Day.* His small library contained books such as, *The Art of War, South Central L.A. Crips, MS-13.* He still had his police training manuals and a book called *Criminal Law, Cases and Comments,* by Fred E. Inbau, James R. Thompson, and Andre A. Moenssens.

When he was at work, I vegged out, watched old movies, and chilled as I figured out my next move.

At Romero's insistence, we drove up the coast to Santa Barbara for a day visit at the Old Missions that were now historical museums. I wore my disguise of a Tina Turner wig and a floppy hat with sunglasses.

The ocean sparkled like a sapphire gem it was so clear that day, and the mountains loomed on the horizon. Birds twittered and fought in the distance. The weather was a perfect eighty degrees, not too hot, or not too cool, just right. The adobe homes and mansions were surrounded by bougainvilleas, geraniums, and oleander. Palm trees of different species flourished in this area. Monarch butterflies floated on the wind and I felt a sense of joy for the first time in years.

For the first time, I was glad I was not an officer anymore. I no longer missed that lifestyle. In fact, I realized something. I liked my life as a private investigator—even if it put me in danger. But I liked living dangerously and free. I decided I could help more people without being part of a bureaucracy.

Romero and I strolled through the Santa Barbara Mission, and we both were overcome by the sense of history. "To think our people settled California," Romero commented, "and now we're the under-classes."

"Well, we've had a black mayor and now we've got a Latino mayor, Villaraigosa, so I guess we're taking Southern California back," I reminded him.

"It won't be soon enough."

"Well, if we want to get technical, the native Americans were here first."

"True." Romero seemed impressed with my knowledge of California history.

We stopped and ate a lunch of linguini and salad at Aldo's Italian Restaurant. While we were eating, Romero brought up the question since Santa Barbara appeared to be predominantly white, and we stood out like black-eyed-peas in a bowl of rice.

"Do you have a problem with me being Latino?"

"No. My father was a black Spaniard of sorts. I guess not."

"Ever dated a Mexican or a white guy?" Romero had his usual amused grin on his face.

"No. How 'bout you? Ever dated a black girl?"

Romero smiled. "My ex-wife is black."

I didn't know why this made me feel more comfortable with him but it did. No wonder he knew how funny we black women can act about our hair. He'd begged me to go swimming in his in-ground pool, and I'd declined several times.

That afternoon, we strolled along the coastline, enjoying the breeze of the ocean, the chaparrals and sandstone outcrops. We drove back home that evening after the traffic cleared up.

As we were driving back to Silver Lake, Romero asked me, "When you were on the force, did anyone ever approach you and ask you to do anything illegal?"

"Why do you ask that?" I felt a little irritated.

"I'm just trying to figure out why someone would want to shoot you."

"That's the risk that goes with the job."

"No, I was just wondering if you'd made any enemies."

"No more than most cops make on the street."

"How about Okamoto? Did he have a lot of enemies?"

"None that I knew of." I thought about what Lawrence Collins had told me about two other police appearing on the scene, but I decided not to share this information with him. "Well, at least no more than most cops would have on the streets."

"Do you think there was someone he locked up who wanted to get back at him?"

"No. He'd never mentioned anyone."

"Do you know an undercover cop they call Flag?"

My heart lurched when he said that. I paused. "Yes. Why?" I wondered what he'd heard.

"How well do you know him?"

"This is none of your business, but I used to date him."

For a while Romero became quiet. I wanted to tell him about the disc and what Okamoto had told me the night he died, but for some reason, I held back. We drove the rest of the way to his home in silence.

"How about if we run up to Palm Springs for the weekend?" Romero asked me on Thursday.

At first, I was surprised. "No, I don't think that's a good idea."

"Why don't you live a little?" Romero teased. "Be spontaneous. Life is short."

No." I was adamant.

"Humor me," Romero said. "You're safe with me. Look, I work all the time, and I never take advantage of all the fun right in my own back yard here in L.A."

Reluctantly, I gave in. In the back of my mind, I thought about my investigation for Trayvon, and how angry Chica was at me, and I felt guilty. But, then again, I thought about it. If someone killed me, I wouldn't be able to investigate Trayvon's death, so maybe I needed to just sit still for a moment and see what the police could do. Maybe the police could handle this better than me. Maybe I was out of my league. I didn't have a badge and L.A.P.D. behind my name anymore. I was out there on my own.

I told myself, "I'll get back on it when it's safe to go home." But the truth of the matter was, I was enjoying Romero's company. We laughed easily together, and we were having a good time, in spite of the circumstances.

I thought about how I could've died when I was shot, and then I changed my mind. I liked this space I was in. I wanted, even if just for a moment, to escape all my worries about Trayvon, Okamoto, Mayhem, Venita. I didn't want to have to worry if someone was trying to harm me. In fact, I hadn't even worried about taking a drink since I'd taken a moment to relax.

Although I was against going to Palm Springs, I gave in. I was going to start living *la vida loca*.

28

As surprised as I was when Romero invited me to Palm Springs, I still kept my guard up. I continued to wear a wig, sunglasses and a hat pulled down low when I left his house. All week I'd made most of my AA meetings. I guess I could make it without a meeting for two days. So far, taking a drink was the farthest thing from my mind in this environment. I had to admit it was nice having a man's company.

I thought of the ways Romero was like me, somewhat of a loner, and how he was different. He was much calmer, laid back. He seemed calm at all times. He had a coolness, a mystique about him.

We drove to Palm Springs on Friday and returned on Sunday. The desert had always been a high energy, spiritual place for me, and I could feel myself draining away all the grief, all the pain, all the hurt of the last year the farther we got away from L.A. As Romero drove at a good seventy-five miles per hour on the open highway, the sand dunes, the mountains, the sage, and sable, the orange and pink cliffs, whirred past my car window and relaxed me.

We checked in a Marriott hotel without a reservation, because summer time was the slow season for Palm Springs. The room had two large beds, and it was understood that we were not to sleep together. Inside, I was feeling conflicted about this. For one, I was beginning to feel Romero. I liked his manliness, his sense of assuredness and self-possession.

That first evening, we drove to an El Salvador restaurant set right out in the middle of the desert and
ordered plantains and black bean and corn-filled tortillas.

The center of the table was set with fresh oranges
and lemons surrounded by scented candles. The place
boasted a combination of world foods, from middle
Eastern and Mediterranean and African cuisine. The
fragrance of ginger, cinnamon, cumin, mint, olive, tur-
meric, parsley and sesame seed filled the restaurant. At
the end of the meal, the waiter provided us with sweet
mint tea.

The average temperature was one hundred and ten
in the dessert. We tried to go for a walk to browse
through the shops, but we wound up having to try to
tiptoe between businesses to get up under their air con-
ditioning systems.

When we made it back to our hotel, we took a dip in
the hotel's pool. I didn't bring a bathing suit, so I cut off
a pair of jeans and swam in shorts and a T-shirt.

"Ooohh, wee. Ooo, la-la, wee, wee," Romero let out a
long, wolf- call whistle at my figure, which bordered on
thick now. He blew his fingers like I was too hot to trot,
which made me blush. I hurried and dipped into the
water, which felt refreshing due to the heat.

Romero jumped in right behind and started dunking
me, teasing me, and splashing me. Between the water,
and the playing around, I could feel things heating up
between us. As he tried to kiss me in the water, I pulled
away though.

He acted as if nothing had happened, and continued
to play around.

"Let me rub your feet," Romero offered, after we got
back to the room to shower and change back into our
clothes.

I just laid back and relaxed as Romero massaged my feet, my shoulders, my hands, my scalp. He used this good smelling lavender oil, which went deep into my skin and healed. A sense of peace washed over me and I surrendered to the flow. I felt as if I was swirling up into the darkness, far, far away.

The next morning I lay in bed, relaxed, spent and satisfied. I'd just had the most satisfying series of multiple orgasms that I'd ever had in my life. And what surprised me the most was the sex didn't include a lot of freaky, crazy stuff like handcuffs and whips.

In fact, I had to hold back, to hide what a freak I'd become from Romero. I just followed his lead and everything was so good. I'm so glad we didn't get into the kinky things I'd done with Flag, which always left me feeling cheap afterwards. I felt good about myself in the light of morning today. We were just a man and a woman making passionate love. Not just two desperate people pushing the envelope, and not always in a good way.

I lay there, evaluating Romero, trying to think of what had been so different and why I felt so moved. Generally, as a cop, I learned to be as callous as the men I worked with, so I didn't have time to "fall in love."

Even so, I couldn't help but compare Romero's style of lovemaking to Flag's. Flag was all about technique, but there was no love in him. Ironically, I really felt a lot of love coming through from Romero, and his technique, as a result, seemed even better. He'd been considerate and made sure he had condoms, versus me having to tell him to use one.

"You're sure you're not on Viagra?" I teased him when he was ready to go a fourth round back to back.

He looked down at his package. "Mami, this is all you. I've waited a long time for this moment."

Thinking of it, Flag could take his selfish behind ass and go take a long leap off a short bridge. If his name is on the list of officers on the take, he's not the type of person I'd want to ever be in my space again.

Now with Romero—he'd just showed me what love-making was about. He made love like poetry. His love felt like words with a rhythm, a motion, a passion, and a sound—all communicating a deeper meaning behind them. I no longer looked at him as an adversary. He was the man.

At the same time, I was not trying to read more into it than it was, but last night Romero whispered he loved me. I didn't say anything back. Was it too soon?

"You know I wasn't supposed to get intimate while I'm in recovery."

"Okay, we won't do it again," Romero teased.

I took my pillow and hit him with it and we started a pillow fight, which wound up being another passionate tango of arms, legs, tongues, and body parts.

"I hope you don't think I'm easy," I said afterwards, as we lay spooned in each other's arms. I stared down at his olive hand clasping my dark hand.

"Easy? This has only been fifteen years since we met and since I've wanted to make love to you."

On the way back from Palm Springs, headed to Silver Lake, I asked Romero to stop at Okamoto's house in La Puente. It was along the way off the 10 San Bernadino Freeway. I just had a hunch.

Earlier in the week, I'd called his ex-wife, Laura, and she told me that Okamoto's house was still on the market. According to Laura, Okamoto died without a will, so the house was still caught up in probate.

We stopped in La Puente. For a while we sat on the street and studied the house. It was at the end of a cul-de-sac. The grass had grown waist-high tall and Okamoto's bungalow house was boarded up. I thought back to how neat he kept his lawn and how proud he was of his two-bedroom and I almost cringed.

"Well, let's see if we can get in," I suggested.

"You know this is trespassing, Z," Romero remarked. "Do you know what we're looking for?"

"I don't know. I thought Okamoto was my friend, and there was something he wanted to tell me the night he was killed, but he never got to tell me. Maybe I can find out what it is if we can look around his house." I knew I was only telling part of the truth. I really didn't know what it was I wanted to find out.

With Romero's agreement, we went around to the back. As it was Sunday, the neighbors were home. One freckled face, red haired man about in his thirties came over.

"What do you want?" the neighbor asked.

Romero flashed his badge. The neighbor backed up. "I'm sorry," he said sheepishly, and shuffled back to his house.

We found a loose board in the back window where his sliding glass door used to be. Romero moved aside the shattered glass, and we stepped inside.

The once immaculate house was turned upside down. All the furniture had been turned over, and ransacked.

When Romero didn't get up and call the police, something inside me made me think I could trust him. I figured someone had been here looking for the disc, so this disc was important enough for them to break in. Somebody was aware of its existence and it was probably someone who was on that disc.

"Here," I said, pushing a copy of Okamoto's disc. "They were probably looking for this."

"What is this?" Romero looked puzzled.

I gave him a copy of the disc.

"I don't know who I can trust. This CD has incriminating information that could put my life in danger worse than what I've gone through looking into Trayvon's death. This tape belonged to Okamoto. You have to be careful who you give it to. I hope I'm doing the right thing."

29

That Monday Romero called me from work. "Guess what, Mami?"

I smiled inwardly, liking how he called me, "Mamacita." Or "Mami" since we'd made love in Palm Springs. I guess we were somewhat of a couple now.

"Yes, what, babe?"

"We have a suspect in custody for Trayvon's death."

"What?" I almost dropped my phone; I was so excited. "When? Good. Who is it?"

"It's an Enrique Sanchez. He's an undocumented immigrant from Guatemala."

"Does any one put him on the scene of the crime?"

"Yes. We've got several eyewitnesses.

"Well, I guess I can go on home."

"No, please stay a little longer. I'll be home by noon. I'm taking off. We should celebrate."

I sucked my teeth in reply. "No, things are cool now. I just thought someone was after me for asking questions about Trayvon and that they might follow me home and hurt Shirley, Chill, and the girls.

"Besides, I need to get home. Chica's wedding is coming up next week and I've got to get my bridesmaid dress."

"Did you turn in the disc?"

"I'll tell you when I get home."

I wanted to ask Romero if he'd heard anything about two unknown police officers being the shooters in the

Okamoto case, and if these persons were still at large, but something made me hold back. I didn't know if this was related to what was on the CD. I decided I would follow up on that investigation when I made it back home.

I called Chica, and this time she answered her phone. "Chica, good news. They have a suspect in custody for Trayvon's murder."

Although she listened to me, Chica did not seem as happy as I'd hoped she would be. She sounded rather flat. I couldn't put my finger on it, but then, who was I to say how a mother would feel about someone who had murdered her child. The suspect's arrest would not bring Trayvon back to life.

After I hung up, I heard Romero's house phone ring and I almost jumped out my skin. I hadn't heard this phone ring during the entire week I stayed with him, but something compelled me to answer it.

A male voice asked, "So she's clean, man?"

I grunted an assent.

"Well, we'll keep a tail on her a while longer for her own safety."

Mouth wide open, I hung up. What the F—? Who was following me? Who was Romero? Did I really know this man? Who was he with? Was he a FED? A DEA officer? Internal Affairs? An undercover detective?

I thought about all the questions Romero had asked me when my guard was down. What a fool I'd been! I could kick my own ass. As I packed, I became so furious, I threw my clothes into my bag, without folding anything. I wanted to go crazy and tear up his place, but I didn't so I sat down and wrote him a brief note.

Romero,

I appreciate this week we spent together, but you didn't have to pretend you were in love.

*Thanks for perpetrating yourself to be some-
one that you're not. I really thought I could trust
you, but I see I can't. Drop my number out your
cell phone. Don't ever call me again. –Z*

As soon as I returned home, I got caught up in the
whirlwind of Chica's wedding preparation, which was
a week away, so that helped me forget the little farce
I'd just gone through. I admitted it to myself. I'd been
played. At least with Flag, I always knew he was a fool,
and a straight-up dog, so I didn't worry about any of
his indiscretions. But Romero? I couldn't believe he
turned out to be like all the rest of them and this really
hurt. He had betrayed my trust, and that was worse to
me.

At the same time, I still was worried and had to keep
looking over my shoulder. I was glad they had someone
in custody for Trayvon, but the two shooters for Okamoto and myself were still at large. What was I going to
do if they came after me? I continued to wear a disguise
when I went out, and I tried to stay close to the house
until the dinner party and the wedding.

Meantime, I ignored the twenty text messages and
phone messages from Romero.

Finally, when I answered one of Romero's phone
calls, we had a heated argument.

"Z, we need to talk."

"For what?"

"I need to explain why I had to do what I had to do."

"So you got the CD out of me, but that wasn't enough—
huh?"

"I didn't ask you for the CD. I didn't know it existed,
and I sure didn't know you had it."

"No, you didn't, but you played my with emotions. Or was it you had to see if I was the precinct slut?"

"You know I respect you as a woman."

"Well, besides my husband and one other, I haven't slept around the station. You are so machismo. You want the Virgin Mary. But I feel more used by you than I did by those teenage boys who mugged me when you met me. At least, they knew they were criminals. And even Flag—the whore that he is—never pretended to be nothing more than he was."

"Z, there are a lot of things I'm not at liberty to share with you right now. Please trust me."

"Yeah, I trusted you before and I got screwed. Thanks but no thanks! Don't call me anymore."

30

On the evening of the bridal dinner party at Charley Brown's Restaurant on the water in Marina Del Rey, I noticed Chica seemed antsy. She kept smoothing down her well-fitted champagne colored dress, twisting her hands all evening, and giving vague answers. Her eyes looked clear and her pupils were not dilated so I assumed she was sober.

Come to think of it, Chica had even seemed "spacey" that way a week earlier at her bridal shower, although she received quite a few gifts. I got a little worried, but I pushed those fears aside. "Please don't let her be using," I prayed.

I was also fighting my disappointment about the scrap I had with Romero. I really had wanted him to escort me to the wedding. Now, I was sitting alone, wishing I had a date. Haviland had Trevor, another white boy, by her side and Chica now had Riley.

When I stepped out in the foyer, Riley came up on me. He had a concerned look screwed on his clean-cut face. "Z, can I ask you a question?"

"What is it, Riley?" I asked, holding my back stiff, since I was not comfortable around him yet.

Apparently, Riley was comfortable with me, though. He went right to the point. "Do you think Chica is back on the drugs?"

"No."

He scratched his bare chin. He really looked disturbed and uncertain.

"She seems clean when I'm around her," I added.

"Her tests are always clean, as far as I know."

"Well, then what is it that makes you think she's back on that stuff?"

"She's been sneaking out at night and coming in around two or three in the morning. She's always sweaty, like she's been running. Once I even found blood on her jacket."

"What did she say it came from?"

"She says she cut her hand."

"Did she have a cut on it?"

"Yes, but . . ."

"Don't worry," I assure Riley. "She's all right. She really loves you."

But I began to question everyone I knew. Who was Romero? Did I ever really know him? What made me sleep with him? Did I really feel something for him?

And Haviland, who was acting so Hollywood tonight, she made me sick. Who was she—like really? Tonight I watched her personality go through so many changes, I swore she was like a chameleon. When she was with Chica's Latina friends, she could speak Spanish like them, but when my black friends showed up, she was down with them. When Riley's relatives, who were white, showed up, she was totally Caucasian.

Not to mention, I thought it was mighty funny how Haviland lived in a gated community, and someone managed to do a home invasion robbery while they were at home. It sounded like her insurance paid her a grip for that, too.

That night, Chica spent the night at Shirley's and slept in my apartment.

"Yeah, we don't want to see each other before the wedding," Chica said. "It's bad luck."

Chica's voice didn't even sound right to me. She sounded like a singer who was off-key. Something wasn't right, but I couldn't quite put my finger on it. My gut was roiling and turning, and for once, I listened to it.

We went to bed around ten. Since there was no alcohol at the dinner, we were totally sober. I felt good being sober. I wanted to get up bright and early. I listened as Chica made a big show of yawning, and stretching. "Ooo, I'm zonked," she said.

Although I had on pajamas, I kept a tee shirt and pants under them. I pretended I was knocked out as soon as I lay down. I even snored a little to pull off my ruse.

About twelve o'clock, just when I really was about to doze off, I heard Chica roll off and tiptoe out of her pallet I'd made for her on my living room floor. She had on all black and you really couldn't tell if she was a male or female. She pulled a black cap over her head.

I grabbed my Glock, put it in my waist band, then waited until I heard Chica's car pull off. I climbed in my car and followed her at a safe distance. I was surprised to see her driving east. I had no idea where she was headed. She took the streets, going out King Boulevard over to Alameda then south to Third Street. She made a right and headed for East Los Angeles. The farther east we traveled, a heavy fog started rolling in. I had a hard time keeping up with her, but I kept my eye on her blurry-looking tail lights.

As I followed her, I wondered if I ever knew anyone—really? Who was Shirley? Even my foster mother wasn't who I thought she was. I mean, I never would have thought she would take care of Chill, as bad as their relationship seemed. Or even my birth mother, Venita. I never really knew her. All these years I thought she killed Strange so she wouldn't have to be bothered with us. To finally face the truth that it was my brother who did the shooting. I guess he saved both my mother and me. Well, I still hadn't wrapped my brain around that one yet.

Take Haviland. I was still trying to figure out how masked robbers entered a gated community in Hollywood Hills and robbed my friend. Something was just not right here. It was just not sitting right with my spirit. There was just a psychological dissonance in this for me. I didn't believe it. Like Chill used to say, "Trust your guts." Well, my guts told me there was some shit in the game going on with Haviland and her boyfriend Trevor. If Haviland's place got broken in, then I've got beachfront property. I had a hunch that there was more to that story, too.

Then Romero, who I thought loved me. How he used me—that when I thought I was under protective custody, he was actually investigating me. But why did he cross the line and sleep with me then?

And here Chica was supposed to be getting married the next day, and she was out here acting like she was back on drugs. Acting just like a crack head, sneaking out in the middle of the night. I hoped she was not hooking too, because I knew that she'd done it in the past when she was strung out on that crack. I'd run her Department of Justice record and accosting and soliciting was at the top of the list of her repeat offenses.

I mulled over so many facts that I didn't realize we had been driving almost a half an hour. I continued to trail Chica. She didn't seem to be worried that anyone was on her tail because she never made any quick turns. We crossed the bridge at the foot of downtown and we were now getting near the lip of East Los Angeles. I saw a group of three young men walking on the street.

Chica's rental car, which she said she only rented to come down from the valley to the dinner party, and to spend the night before the wedding, slowed down. I heard her call out to these three young Latino men. What were they doing on the deserted street I wondered

From my car, I couldn't tell their ages, but they looked to be in their early twenties. I couldn't tell if they looked like gang members because so many young men wear the baggy clothes and big jackets. I heard one call back to her in a congenial voice in Spanish, as if they were offering her directions.

The next thing I knew, when the young men approached her car, Chica stepped out, face to face with them, and started to open fire. This was no drive-by. This was a straight-out ambush. From where I was sitting in my car, all I saw was gunfire and the young men hollering and dropping. Apparently, they were unarmed because there was no return gunfire.

I couldn't believe what I just witnessed.

With that, Chica climbed back in her car and pulled off in what seemed like the slowest, leisurely fashion for someone who just committed a crime. She did not drive fast or too slow. Dumbfounded, I sat for a moment and wondered if I should call the police and get help for the young men, or if I should make sure Chica went home, or if I should do a citizen's arrest.

My right hand was shaking so badly, I almost couldn't dial the cell phone when I decided to call 911 and put in an anonymous tip so someone could come help the young men. I didn't wait around though. Some invisible hand forced me to follow Chica. I sped up to catch up with her. She was driving back west towards Shirley's—I hoped.

My mind was whirling like a dervish. What was I going to do? How could I turn in Chica? My sister? My friend? So she was a vigilante now? Was she taking the law into her own hands? Obviously, she was.

After about a half hour, I caught up with her car and I blew my horn. She turned her head and looked over at me, as if she'd never seen me before. I beckoned at her to pull over to the curb. When she recognized me, she finally pulled over to a nearby curb.

I sprinted to her car door and flung it open. I called out Chica's name. She turned as slowly as a wound up clock, then stared at me as if she were looking right through me. As if I weren't even there. A chill charged through me, she looked so strange. Her eyes were glazed over like she was in a trance. She stood there, not flinching a muscle, a zombie.

"Chica? Chica? What have you done?" My voice choked up. "They have a suspect in custody. Why are you doing this? Is this the first time you've done this?"

In a dramatic voice, Chica quoted Shakespeare's Lady Macbeth,

> *Come to my woman's breasts,*
> *And take my milk for gall . . .*

She beat her chest with both fists. "That's right. I did like a man would do. I'm willing to murder—for my son."

For a moment, she fell silent. When she spoke again, she said very simply, "You were taking too long. It's done now. No more killing. I'm a victim no more."

31

We both drove in our separate cars back to Shirley's garage. We got in around three in the morning. I tossed and turned the rest of the night, while Chica snored her ass off like she hadn't done shit.

Before the wedding, I listened to the radio for any news. There was a report, and it sounded like all three young men lived, but were in serious condition. The media was calling this a hate crime. They thought it was gang-related. The young men were not affiliated with any gangs. No one ever mentioned that the shooter was a woman. It was a good thing Chica had a rental car, I thought. And hopefully, when the young men came to, they couldn't identify Chica. Then I caught myself, because I was trying to help her get away with her crime.

Inside, I resented Chica for involving me in this. When you loved someone, their transgressions became your transgressions. Their secrets, your secrets. Their lies, your lies. I'd already decided to carry Venita's and Mayhem's lies to the grave.

The next morning, I kept looking in Chica's face as I helped her dress. I fixed her hair, then helped her adjust her veil.

"Chica, is there anything you want to talk to me about?"

Chica looked at me with this vague smile. "No."

I didn't know what to think. Had Chica lost her freakin' mind? Had I ever really known Chica? Should I report her ass? I didn't know what to do.

The wedding took place at St. Mark's Cathedral, a large Catholic Church on Wilshire Boulevard in Santa Monica since Riley was Catholic. During the candlelight service, I gazed at Chica's face. Instead of looking like a cold-blooded killer, she was looking luminous. A glow shone on her face, as if a gauze of peace had settled over her with these random acts of violence. As if she'd somehow evened out the scores of the universe.

The priest's voice droned on, "Love is long suffering . . ."

My mind half listened. I was torn as to what to do. If I did contact the law, what would I say. How could I snitch on my sister?

"Love is kind . . ."

As the singer got up and sang "Ave Maria" I made up my mind. I'd grown up where you were taught the worse thing in the world was to be a snitch. Even my mother took the rap for her child. I decided I was no snitch, either. Besides, this girl was like a sister to me. I guess I'd just have to live with Chica's secret, too.

I focused on the wedding, which was beautiful. Chica's daughters all wore champagne, ankle-length voile dresses. Chica, whose hair was fluffed around her shoulders, looked like a movie star in Haviland's expensive diaphanous wedding gown. Brooklyn made a beautiful flower girl. She had her hair pulled up in a ponytail sprinkled with baby's breath. A little boy from Shirley's church carried the ring on a silken pillow. Even Daddy Chill stayed mentally straight long enough to walk Chica down the aisle.

The church was decorated in pale gardenias at the end of each pew with white ribbons. Over three hundred people were present, so it was far from a small ceremony.

I guess Chica was getting her wish. She was now the Cinderella bride in her own fairy tale. After the nightmare of a life she'd had, who was I to begrudge her happiness?

Thanks to Haviland, there were little touches such as a modern dancer coming down the aisle, the reading of their vows, the lighting of the candles by the couple, the jumping over the broom, the releasing of the white doves after the service, and instead of throwing rice, throwing confetti at the new couple.

No one seemed to notice what a rainbow wedding this was. Chica, a Chicano, with four surviving biracial daughters, marrying a white dude. Even the people in attendance came from every race under the sun.

After the wedding, the reception was held at a Doubletree Hotel in Santa Monica near the ocean. Haviland and I went and sat outside in the pavilion. Haviland still smoked. Thank goodness I quit the tobacco habit when I stopped drinking.

I didn't know if Haviland was high, but she opened up and admitted something to me. "I feel like my life has been one missing thing. Just that one act of my mother signing a piece of paper is why I'm so disjointed. I hate my adoptive parents and my birth parents. I can't help it. I know my mother is dead, but I haven't forgiven her. Not really . . ." Her voice dropped off for a moment.

"I should forgive her though. She gave me a chance at life. With my adoptive parents being in the industry,

I was able to get into acting at five. I was the child star. Before eighteen, I was voted a triple threat. I was doing acting, singing, modeling. So where did I go wrong? Was it a case of too much too soon?"

"What's the matter, Hav? The wedding was a success. You did a great job. Maybe you should try to become a wedding planner."

Haviland continued to look downhearted. "I have a problem, Z."

"Oh, no. You're not back on the pills, are you?"

"No."

"Then, what is it?"

"You know you've always gave it to me straight. You've been a real friend. I feel I can trust you."

"What is it?"

"It's money problems."

"Who doesn't have them? You're in good company. The whole country is broke. Didn't you get the home insurance money and your mother's insurance?"

She nodded. "But I'm being blackmailed."

"What?" For a moment I was shocked. "Why?"

"I staged that home invasion robbery so that I could get the insurance money to save my house from foreclosure."

"What?" Now I knew why this thing had been bothering me all along. It didn't add up. That's when I knew this girl was scandalous.

"Now the guy that broke in is blackmailing us. I have to pay him money every month."

I didn't know what to say, so I said nothing. I didn't know if weddings were like truth serums, for everyone seemed to be opening up, making confessions at the reception.

Later, at the reception, I even found Shirley opening up to me.

She told me how she met Haviland's adoptive mother. "I first met Ilene at a function for abused and neglected children given in Beverly Hills at a fancy hotel. This is how we became friends. We were an unlikely pair, she was white, I was black, she was rich, I was middle-class or average, not poor, mind you. Although you never met her and Haviland, what we had in common was our two little black girls. I had you and she had Haviland, whom she had adopted as a baby. She would ask me questions about if she should let Haviland go to a black church, or sometimes she would ask me for hairdressers who could work with Haviland's hair.

"Later I got Chica, and you know what a handful she was. I guess Ilene and I kind of lost touch over the years, that is, until Haviland started giving her problem with those drugs. She started back calling me."

It could have been the Moet she drank, but Shirley even told me something she never divulged before. "Did I tell you Chill and I had a baby boy who died shortly after birth back when we first got married?" Her eyes brimmed with tears.

Once again I felt my jaw dropping to the ground. *How many more revelations would this wedding bring?* I thought as I patted Shirley on the back.

"I could never get pregnant again. I wanted lots of babies. That's why I've opened my home for years, even at the expense of my marriage. It seemed like the more children I took in, the farther Chill and I grew apart."

I hadn't thought about how we could have put a strain on her marriage.

"I'm sorry, Moochie."

"No, don't be. I don't care. Like Maya Angelou says, 'I wouldn't trade 'nothing for my journey.' I love you guys. My life would have been empty without you. I'm

the better for having known all you. You have all grown
up to be good people."

"I always had better luck with the girls—at least until Chica. It seems like the boys, I always got them too
late. They would already be heading for juvy. I guess I
felt like God was giving me a second chance when He
gave me Trayvon. I guess that's why he was always my
favorite, and maybe that wasn't right."

I couldn't say anything. There were times there was
nothing to say. I just listened.

The rest of the night flew by and finally the reception
was over. The whole family was staying at the hotel
that night and going to Disneyland the next day, but I
wanted to sort through my thoughts so I drove home
alone.

As I drove home from the wedding reception, sheets
of rain pummeled against my windshield. The skies
turned purple black and I couldn't see well, but I
inched my way carefully along the glassy, oil-slicked
streets. I didn't feel like staying around family, and I
just wanted to be alone with my thoughts. I was still
hurting over Romero. I really hated he didn't make it to
the wedding. I wanted to be alone to nurse my wounds
and review why I was hurting, since I was the one who
broke it off.

Los Angeles was the worse place to drive in inclem-
ent weather since Los Angelenos are so spoiled with our
fair weather. I knew the freeway would be littered with
car accidents so I took the streets versus the freeway,
and when I finally got in from the wedding reception, I
kicked off my heels and slipped into my sweats. It had
been a long day and night. I decided I'd take a shower in
the morning. I stretched out on my futon, almost ready

to konk out. My hands felt frostbitten, they were so cold. I rubbed them together absently, and I thought, *As soon as I warm up, I'm going to sleep.* But my mind wouldn't let me sleep. It kept spinning around and around. I was still bugged out over what Chica did last night. How many times had she gone out like a vigilante before? In the other cases, did the victim or victims die? Why was she shooting Latinos if she was Chicano herself? Was it because a Latino came up and shot her son, her baby, who was black in appearance? Mothers did do crazy things. I shook my head. I didn't know anything anymore.

I finally began to doze off. I jumped when my cell phone rang, interrupting my slight snooze. I glanced down at the caller ID and realized it was Romero. I planned on telling him off again, and spewing some more of the venom I'd been holding inside.

"What the hell do you want?" I snapped as soon as I spoke into the phone.

"Where are you? Still at the wedding I hope."

"No, I'm at home."

Romero's usually calm voice went ballistic. "Get out of your place. You're in danger."

"What are you talking about? Stop playing, Romero."

"Flag is coming over there to kill you. There's a hit out on your life. He and Anderson killed Okamoto and accidentally killed Trayvon. Anderson did the shooting on Trayvon, because he thought it was you since you'd been catching the bus. Now they're coming to finish you off."

My heart started doing jumping jacks. "What? Why? What do they want with me?"

"They know you have Okamoto's CD. I've already turned my copy over to the FBI and Internal Affairs. Must be a mole in the department because it's been leaked to them. They want to get rid of you as a witness. I'm headed there now, and I've called a squad car for back up. Get the hell outta there!"

My heart was beating so fast, I could hardly move. I guess what really froze me in my spot was the dead glare of the two men standing in my apartment, holding me at gunpoint.

"Okay, got you," I said quietly, clicking my phone shut.

"Were you going somewhere?" a familiar voice inquired.

I stopped dead in my tracks. Flag was the voice's owner. There stood Flag and Officer Anderson, the white sidekick from the 77th Division of the Los Angeles Police Department. So this was L and M.

They were both dressed in black and holding, respectively, .38 caliber guns and a 9 mm gun. They had silencers on their guns.

Their guns and my churning gut informed me this was not a social call, but I tried to play it off. "Hey, Flag. Anderson, I assume? What are you doing in my spot?'

"Z," Anderson said bluntly, eyes narrowing with contempt. "We want that disc."

"What disc are you talking about?" That's when I started praying. *Higher Power, God, help me. I've got too much to live for.*

"The one that Okamoto gave you."

"He didn't give me anything." I turned to Flag and decided to buy some time, even appeal to his human decency. "Flag, I never took you for a killer. After all we've been through together."

"Yeah, you sure are—were a good lay. I'm going to miss you, but we ain't been hooking up lately no way."

"Aw cut the bullshit and the love talk, Flag," Anderson spat out. He turned back to me, as if reasoning with a child. "Now, we can kill you before or after we get the disc—it's up to you."

I decided to stall for time. "So is this what it comes to—hey, Flag? After all we meant to each other. You know I love you."

I could see Flag begin to vacillate between wanting to do the right thing, but being too far in to turn back. "I didn't shoot your nephew, Z. I swear to God. That was an accident. It was a mistake. I didn't mean for that to happen."

"Well, who shot him then?"

"I did," Anderson said boldly. "I thought it was you. This time I'll make sure I don't miss."

"Are you L and M?"

"Yeah, that was our undercover names. So what?" Anderson snapped.

"Did you steal the Mexican Mafia's drugs?"

"What's it to you?"

"So you purposely wanted the blacks and the Latinos to be pitted against each other? Is that right, Anderson?"

"So what? The spics and the niggas can kill each other off for all I care."

"Flag, you gon' let him talk about you like that? Did you hear him use the 'N' word?" I decided to try to divide and conquer.

"Yeah, man. Watch your mouth. You know I don't play that shit." Flag sounded irritated, and I noticed his eyes were off me. I tried to inch over to my purse, which was about two feet away on a night stand.

"Man, don't you see what she's doing?" Anderson snapped. He turned back to me. "Now do you have that disc?"

I had to think fast. "Here it is, in my purse." This time I was only a foot away from my purse.

Anderson bolted across the little room to grab my purse, but I reached my clutch purse in time and pulled out my pearl handled Glock and fired it, hitting him dead between the eyes. Before Flag could react, Ben, who was usually in hiding, broke out from under the futon and tripped Flag up.

"What the hell was that?" Flag was muttering. "You've got rats? I hate rats! Shit!"

In that moment that it took him to get his bearings, I turned on him. Although Flag fired his gun first from floor-level, he missed both Ben and me. In that split second, I fired back, hitting him in the chest, and taking him out.

"That's for Trayvon and Okamoto," I said, feeling a sanguine satisfaction. I placed my smoking gun back in my purse. Now I could see why Chica seemed so at peace at her wedding. Payback was a bitch.

My apartment had become a virtual bloodbath, but thank God, it was not my blood this time. I hugged Ben, and rubbed his fur. "Thank you."

Ben gave me that squinty-eyed look that made me feel like we communicated. I picked him up and left my apartment. I put him in my car, and I climbed in the driver's seat.

The wail of police sirens screaming in the background passed me as I drove west, away from my garage, and as I called Romero, I knew help was on the way.

Epilogue

Six months later . . .

"G-Ma, have you seen my hair brush?" Malibu asked Shirley. "I told Soledad to leave my stuff alone."

"I didn't take your brush," Soledad retorted. "You make me sick." She stuck out her tongue.

"Okay, girls, stop fussing." Shirley frisked her hands like "hurry, hurry." "We've got to get to the rally."

We were preparing to go to a rally where we would meet with a group of over one hundred mothers who'd lost family members to street violence. This was a nonprofit group who was organizing and providing resources for Mothers of Murdered Children.

We were getting dressed and everyone was excited. The other day we'd dropped Trayvon's clothes at the Goodwill—something we needed to do for closure, according to the children's family therapist.

Everyone was here, except Chica and Riley and Haviland and Trevor. They were running late and would meet us at the rally.

Chica had decided to leave the children with Shirley and just do weekend visits every week to keep from further disrupting the girls' lives. They both decided to share custody—almost like a divorce case—with a legal guardianship court order that did not terminate Chica's parental rights.

As for me, I was feeling content because I had Romero at my side. He leaned over and gave me a big kiss. "You all right?"

I kissed him back. "Right as rain."

I was proud to say, I just received my ribbon for my first year anniversary of sobriety at my AA meeting yesterday. Romero came to the meeting and stood up and clapped for me.

I was so happy that I was staying sober, that I was beginning to like myself. Some days it was still a struggle, particularly after a hard case. I'd finally accepted that drinking would always be a problem for me. I would never wake up one day and say, "I'm cured. I'm not an alcoholic anymore."

When I was on the force, it was like a knee-jerk reaction for me to take a drink at the end of a bad shift. In order to stay sober now, I followed Joyce's advice. I tried not to get too tired, too stressed, too hungry. I would have to continue to deal with this demon the rest of my life, one day at a time.

So much had happened since I took down Flag and Anderson. Lawrence Mitchell was released from jail before his case had a chance to go to trial, and the charges were dropped. The suspect from Guatemala whom they'd arrested in Trayvon's murder case was also released, but he was deported as he was undocumented.

I guess I never completely knew Okamoto, but he was a man who would not be bribed. As wasted as he would get on his off days, Okamoto was a man of integrity.

Okamoto's CD, which I gave Romero, apparently took down a lot of folks in high places. Okamoto had been a computer buff, and a hacker, accidentally got into an FBI security frame, passed the security clearance, downloaded the files, then started asking questions. When Anderson and Flag found out he had incriminating information on them and their involvement with the drugs they stole from the Mexican Cartel, it came down to either him or them.

I guess I just got caught up in the mix. I think that's what Okamoto wanted to tell me the night he died. Anyhow, that's why Flag and Anderson followed us and shot us after we transported the children to "Unca Pookie's"—Lawrence Collins. They figured since he had a record, it would be easy to pin the shootings on him.

Later, when Flag came to my house during my binge, he was sent to assassinate me, but he really didn't want to. Instead, he tore up my house, looking for the CD. After he couldn't find the CD, he felt like I didn't know anything and didn't pose a threat to them—particularly as drunk as I was. I can't imagine the tension that probably developed between him and Anderson over him not killing me. Anyhow, I know the only thing that saved me during my drunken periods was grace.

I guess the other factor that backed the two men off of me momentarily was that Internal Affairs seemed to be laying low. They probably thought the heat was off them for the drug corruption investigation.

After I moved in with Shirley, I purposely lost contact with Flag and changed my cell phone. During the time I didn't have a car, they couldn't trace me on the computer, but Anderson, for some reason, was still determined to get rid of me—just in case. Somehow, he found out I was catching the bus. He went after me and shot Trayvon by mistake. For a while, they laid low during the media frenzy over Trayvon's murder, but when they found out I was digging into the case, Anderson started following me.

Just like F-Loc said, "This thing went up to the top."
Judges, some of the top brass at the force, and a
dozen politicians had to step down rather than do time
as a result of the information on the CD. A few big shots
wound up serving time anyhow. This thing was neither
a white or black or brown thing. It was a green thing.
Green with a capital G for greed. Venality. Like the
song goes, "What will you do for money?"

A bright spot in my life was Romero though. After I
shot Flag and Anderson, Romero helped me get out of
any criminal actions against me, in the name of self-
defense. The fact he was able to exonerate me when he
gave up the information on Flag and Anderson's theft
of the confiscated drugs from the Mexican Mafia also
helped our relationship. In time, he and I slowly made
up.

Romero opened up and explained he was part of a
task force operation sent to find corruption within the
force, and although he was checking me out for crime
to see if I'd been dirty when I was a cop, he found out
I was straight. Because I was still tied to Okamoto's
death, unbeknownst to me, I had been under investigation as well to see if I'd set him up. If the task force had
found any wrongdoing on my part, they would have
pressed criminal charges against me as a civilian.

"You know, I figured you were innocent all along,"
Romero said. "And since you were, I always knew the
guilty parties would eventually come back after you
this was one of the hardest things I ever had to do," he
admitted. He apologized profusely for having to lie to
me like that, but it was all in the line of duty.

Since we'd grown closer, Romero admitted he knew
that Mayhem was my brother and that he knew about
his criminal background. But similarly, he was kin to
a large Mexican cartel drug family as well. He under-

stood the family code ran deep on both sides. Maybe we had more in common than we thought. We were both the first in our families to try to live on the right side of the law.

The down side of my life was I still hadn't found my younger siblings, but I hadn't given up trying. I signed up on the adoption registry if they wanted to make contact, but so far, I hadn't heard anything from them. My mother, Venita, and I still had a shaky relationship, but, as they say, "It is what it is."

By the way, my Soldano Investigations Agency was growing and I'd recently gone from being a home-based business to getting a little office in Santa Monica. I had to hire an assistant too—Chica. She was really good at tracking down people. To that end, she was planning on becoming a bounty hunter.

"Hey, Chica. Hey, Z." I looked up to see who was calling our names. Fashionably late as usual, looking Hollywood as ever in her designer shades, Haviland, with Trevor at her side, made a dramatic entrance. She blew fake kisses and handed out autographs to anyone who recognized her.

Chica and I gave each other a look. We broke out laughing. "Hey, Haviland," Chica called out. "You know you're rocking that outfit."

Even Chica had learned to accept Haviland for who she was.

In between small acting gigs and community plays, Haviland had become a wedding planner for some of the rich and famous. Her business was growing due to her clientele's frequent serial marriages. Unfortunately, she still had to pay off her blackmailer every month, but that's Haviland. What could I say?

I looked back on my life and now I didn't just see the darkness I used to see. I saw light. In a crazy way,

Romero had changed my life. Now, I saw love as a possibility and not something that was just a fairy tale.

We all have scars and I guess this was a time for healing. As part of reconnecting with my father's people, I was planning a trip—my first one—to Belize next summer.

One day, when I was at the ocean with Romero, I had an epiphany. Although I was no longer physically trapped in the ghetto, I was mentally trapped because I was a product of it. When I became a cop, I drank to drown out the memories of the sights I saw on the streets, as well as the memories from my own past. But until I confronted my past, I could not face my future. I learned another thing. We could not choose our family, but we could choose the way we wanted to live. Yes, we do have a choice about that.

At the end of the "Mothers of Murdered Children" ceremony, we all released a white balloon in the memory of our loved ones—generally a child. As I released my balloon, I felt like I was releasing all the pain from the past.

I was smiling, feeling content, when suddenly my cell phone rang. I reached in my purse to retrieve it. At first I didn't recognize the voice since there was so much racket from the crowd.

I covered my ear and leaned down, trying to block out the noises from the rally.

"What? Who is this?"

Finally, I recognized the voice. It was Venita and she sounded distraught. Each word she uttered, dropped a bomb on my otherwise peaceful day.

"Mayhem's been kidnapped. They're holding him for ransom."

Book Club Questions

1. What did you think of the chance meeting between Romero and Z during the L.A. riots? Do you believe it was fate? Do you think their interracial relationship stands a chance—given they come from warring crime families?

2. Do you think becoming a police officer was a good choice for Z?

3. Do you think the warring factions between the Los Angeles black and Latino gangs were drug-related or turf-related?

4. When Z became an alcoholic, given her childhood background and the trauma of getting shot, did this make her weak?

5. Did you think Shirley was a good foster mother? Why or why not?

6. Do you think Chica and her fiancé, Riley, both being former substance abusers, have a chance at a happy life?

7. Were you surprised by Chica's actions the night before her wedding?

8. Did you think Haviland was telling the truth about the home invasion robbery she supposedly experienced?

9. Do you think childhood traumas, such as the one Z went through on the night her father was murdered, can be blocked out your mind?

10. What did you think of the shared secret between Z and her Kingpin brother, Mayhem?

Notes

Notes

Notes

Notes